CW00507885

HEARTS ON FIRE
SWEETER THAN PIE

Dixie Lynn Dwyer

MENAGE EVERLASTING

Siren Publishing, Inc.
www.SirenPublishing.com

A SIREN PUBLISHING BOOK
IMPRINT: Ménage Everlasting

HEARTS ON FIRE 4: KISSES SWEETER THAN PIE
Copyright © 2014 by Dixie Lynn Dwyer

ISBN: 978-1-63258-499-1

First Printing: December 2014

Cover design by Les Byerley
All art and logo copyright © 2014 by Siren Publishing, Inc.

Printed in the U.S.A.

PUBLISHER
Siren Publishing, Inc.
www.SirenPublishing.com

DEDICATION

Dear readers,

Thank you for purchasing this legal copy of *Kisses Sweeter Than Pie*.

Dreams can come true, no matter what the obstacles, no matter how hard others try to put you down, minimize your dreams, or attempt to squash them entirely with their negativity. Anything worthwhile in life takes determination, strength, and passion. There's a hunger in each and every one of us who seek that dream, that goal, that almost unreachable, tangible or intangible object of our desires. The difference between those who actually achieve it and reach that goal, that dream, and those that give up, weaken under the power of others' negativity, is that inner strength. The motivation, determination, and hunger that make us thrive to succeed.

Nina is a great example of a woman who has failed, been held down, held back, controlled, manipulated, and oppressed by a man who knows and thrives on the ability to do so.

It takes three men with compassion, with scars of their own, and a deep belief in Nina's beauty and abilities to help Nina to see that the fight is still on, that a new life, achieving her dreams and goals, is within reach with the help of true friends, honest Samaritans, and ultimately true love.

I hope you enjoy her journey.

Happy reading.

Hugs!

~Dixie~

HEARTS ON FIRE 4: KISSES SWEETER THAN PIE

DIXIE LYNN DWYER

Prologue

"I don't have the money, Rico. Please, give me time and I will pay you back."

"You can't pay me back. You owe Xavier thirty grand and now you owe me a hundred grand. I want my fucking money." Rico stared at the old man. He'd seen him gambling for years, his habit costing him more and more just like every other shithead's habit or obsession. Tonight he fucked up. Tonight the old man gambled against Rico and now Rico would get exactly what he was after.

"Do you have my money or not?" Rico asked the old man.

"No. You know I don't. I should have won that last hand," the man said, raising his voice as he looked around the room at the other players and Rico's bodyguards. No one would support him. They all knew what Rico wanted. Her.

"What are you trying to say, that Rico cheated?" Miguel, one of Rico's cohorts, asked.

The old man scrunched his eyebrows together. "You know he cheated. He had that ace up his sleeve. This game was fixed from the start."

Miguel grabbed the old man by the neck and squeezed his throat. The old man would be no match for Miguel, for any of them. Rico walked closer. His confidence and the knowledge he had that his plan was successful fed his next sentence. The old man had no choice.

"There's one way we can work this out. One way only."

The old man looked at him, swallowing with difficulty because of Miguel's professional throat hold.

"What?" he squeaked.

"I will release you of your debt, including the debt you owe Xavier, for one tiny, little thing." Rico thought about Nina. She was petite, sweet, and a virgin with a body of a sexual fantasy. He wanted her just like a lot of the guys in the neighborhood did, but she wasn't biting. He kept his distance, waited for an opportunity, hoping his reputation would never reach her pretty little ears. He looked at the old man.

"What is it? Whatever it is, I'll do it. I have nothing. This was my last bet, my last chance to win big and pay off the debts."

Rico smiled softly. "I want Nina."

The old man's eyes widened and he shook his head side to side profusely. "No. No," he said, practically crying.

Miguel squeezed the old man's throat a little tighter to get his message across.

"That's not the right answer. You give me her, you get her for me, and neither of you will die."

* * * *

Nina Valone took a deep breath as she held the doorknob.

This was a huge risk she was taking. Never in her twenty-four years of life had she been so brazen, so filled with emotion that she allowed those emotions to direct her actions.

Rico is not cheating on me. I've been with him for nearly a year. He was my first lover. My only lover. I won't find him in his apartment with another woman. I won't. What the others told me can't be true. He couldn't have been seen at the club with Stacy. Rico wouldn't do that to me. He loves me. He wants me to achieve my goals, my dreams.

Nina took a deep breath and released it. She thought about how they met. How he saw her through the crowded club, locked gazes with her, and knew they were meant to be. He told her he spotted her. She was sitting all alone. Turning down guy after guy who wanted to buy her a drink, try to cop a feel, or even convince her to go home with them. She turned them all down but then Rico showed up. He acted sweet, funny, and sincere. He didn't even try to touch her, and she found herself wanting him, too.

But that was in the beginning. He'd changed so much. His temper flared often, and he used his strength on her and snapped at her all the time. She wondered if he was getting tired of her. Wondered if he wanted to break up with her. The thought caused a terrible ache in her gut. Without Rico she had no one. Cleo, the closest thing to a guardian she had, died. He died months before she met Rico.

Sadness filled her eyes. Her gut told her that once she opened this door, her life was going to change. Fear gripped her next and she squeezed the knob to the door tight, half wanting to jiggle it, make the noise and alert Rico that she'd arrived back early. It would save her the heartache of actually seeing him in bed with another woman.

God, it felt like shit to be cheated on and used. She never thought she would be in this position. All his words, his sweet talk of commitment and security, were bullshit. She'd fallen for it because she was so damn naive, lonely, and desperate for attention. He said all the right things, and she knew in the beginning that she wasn't the only woman he flirted with or shared time with. But she thought he was committed to her fully once he started seeing her steadily. Once they made love and he proclaimed his commitment and near obsession with her. She swallowed hard. Was this what men did? Manipulated women's minds to make them feel like they were special and important while they cheated, lied, and continued to do whatever they wanted with no thoughts of a woman's emotions and true commitment?

"Stick with me, baby, and I'll get you your own little bakery. You can make all those sweet delicious pies all day long and people will line up down the block for a taste."

Liar!

Her body was shaking. She was the least confrontational person alive. She was a pushover, hence why at twenty-four here she stood outside her boyfriend's door ready to bust him for cheating when only a week ago he was talking engagement rings and establishing a storefront for her pie-making business.

Her eyes welled up with tears. Her stomach began to feel queasy. She wanted to puke.

Hell, she knew he was in there with someone. Was it the redhead from the bar down near his club? Or perhaps the brunette whom he always kissed hello whenever they went to Marcello's Italian cuisine two blocks across from the train station? She thought about it. They were both super pretty, assertive, really experienced, and Nina was a virgin. Well, not anymore. Not since two months into their relationship when she gave it to Rico as he pledged his undying love for her.

"Sap! Men eat little girls for snacks, Nina." She could hear her mother's words. The venom she spewed from her mouth since Nina was five and could understand never left her memory. She was long gone, strung out, perhaps dead in her forties. Nina had nothing but bad memories of her mother. She was surprised that Cleo hung around as long as he did. Her mom's boyfriend of many years took Nina under his wing. He felt bad for her, and he figured out real fast that Sheila Valone was no saint.

If not for Cleo, I'd be dead. I never would have survived foster care.

Suddenly the door opened, along with a sickening little giggle and Rico's soothing, sexy words as he kissed the woman. "That was real good, sweetness."

"Anytime, Rico. You just call me and I'll get here fast."

Nina could practically hear her heart racing. Her palms were sweaty, her stomach ached terribly. She could hear it rumbling as she laid her hand over her belly. Just then Rico and the redhead, the one from the bar near his club called Rick's, noticed her standing there like a frozen statue.

"Nina, what are you doing here?" he asked, his dark eyebrows scrunching together, his lips firm, and the anger apparent on his face as if she were at fault. That was typical Rico. She knew he was going to twist this around. Nina looked at the redhead who just stared at Nina and gave her the once-over. Nina's stomach churned some more.

"Hey, Rico, I thought you were done with her? You stole her little cherry and kicked her out so I can move in," the redhead said, sounding so smug.

Rico grabbed Nina's arm and hissed at the redhead. "Cool it, Stacy. I'll deal with her. I'll call you later."

Nina couldn't believe that this was happening. Right here, before her very eyes, these two acted like she was lower than dirt and didn't matter. *The nerve of her to say that Rico just wanted my virginity. Did he?*

The wheels in her head began to spin. Recollections of past moments of doubt about this relationship, about Rico, entered her mind. She had been young, naive, and impressionable. Especially once she lost Cleo. Cleo had gone missing, his body found days later indicating he was killed. It made her realize that she had to succeed in life or she would end up dead, too. The city streets would eat her alive. It was harder than she thought to find work and establish a career with only a high school diploma.

She glanced at the two people mumbling something. Were they talking about her still, and in a negative fashion? She felt tiny, minuscule, and worthless. Nina's vision blurred. She feared she might pass out as perspiration reached her brow and her stomach continued to rumble. The redhead pushed her tight-fitting black tube dress down further but it didn't matter. If the woman bent forward a few inches, the world would see her goods.

"She's such a pushover."

"Leave her alone, Stacy. I got this," Rico said.

Stacy looked down at Nina. "You're a waste. Being all sweet and innocent is boring. No man like Rico, a man who likes action in bed, the rough stuff, would take someone like you seriously."

The redhead's words pounded inside Nina's head. She thought about the fantasies Rico shared with Nina in bed. He wanted to tie her up, dress her in some sexy leather outfits, and whip her ass and her pussy with some sort of thingy.

She turned to look at Stacy.

"What is wrong with her? Are you deaf or something?"

Nina's head was spinning. She was utterly sick over this, disgusted with Rico, with Stacy, and mostly with herself for sticking around Rico so long.

"She's such a loser. Get rid of her, Rico," Stacy said, giving Nina a flick with her fingers and tapping her stomach. Nina lost it.

The anger hit her head with a throbbing headache, but then her upset over finding out how disloyal and unfaithful Rico truly was overwhelmed her emotions and her body. She threw up all over Stacy.

"Jesus!" Rico blurted out and jumped backward into the apartment. Stacy screamed and stomped her high heels and Nina covered her mouth and ran into the apartment. She could hear Rico yelling at Stacy to get lost and Stacy carrying on. Nina's head was spinning, her heart was aching. She felt like such a loser. She ran into the bathroom and held on to the toilet but nothing more came. She tried to calm her breathing and not focus on what just happened. She thought about Stacy's dress, her smug expression turning to absolute shock and disgust, and Nina found herself laughing.

Then the tears fell. The emotions flooded her body and the crazy thoughts invaded her mind. *Rico doesn't love me. He used me for my body. I'm his possession, his plaything, and I'm not the only one sharing his bed. Yuck.*

The door slammed open.

She turned to see Rico in only his black silky dress pants. The belt undone, no shirt, tan skin, muscles, and his gold crucifix. She used to love the man's body and wonder why he wanted her when all these women wanted him. She had been stupid.

"What the fuck, Nina?" he yelled and hit her. The backhand came so fast and so hard she fell to the left and hit her cheek on the porcelain bathtub.

She was shocked. Outraged. He'd never laid a hand on her before. Always forceful, he kept her close at all times. He tended to be jealous of other men looking at her, which made her feel good inside that he thought her so beautiful and was concerned that another would take her from him. But that wasn't the case.

Before she could register what was happening Rico was pulling her by her hair, dragging her from the bathroom. She had never been so scared, so frightened by a man's anger before. She'd pushed him to his limit and he was the one who was caught cheating.

"Rico, please. Stop it, don't do this. What did I do?" she asked, half covering her face.

"You showed up here when you're supposed to be at work. This is my place, my apartment."

"You're cheating on me?" she asked, tears flowing.

"What the fuck? This is my business. You do as I say. I own your ass, Nina."

"No. No, you don't. You're my boyfriend. We've been together for months now."

"Fuck, Nina, you're my regular lay. There are others. Are you that fucking dense? Do you really think there was only you?"

He bent down and stared at her. She could see the anger in his eyes. She didn't want him to hit her again. She just needed to see if they could work it out. She had no one, no place to go. The deep, desperate feeling of abandonment like she had when she realized her mother didn't love her or care filled her body. Her gut clenched. Why did every person in her life she counted on fail her, give up on her, and just toss her out like garbage? She was a good person, hard worker, and caring, yet they still thought so little of her. She didn't want to be alone. She wanted love, she wanted a man's arms around her at night caring for her and protecting her the way it was supposed to be. But it seemed that was not reality, only fantasy. She needed to try and calm Rico. He was so pissed off.

"Rico, Rico, please tell me what I did wrong? I never cheated on you, so why would you cheat on me?"

His eyes widened. "You're fucking right you never cheated. You're mine. You ever fuck another man, hell, kiss another man, and I'll fucking beat you and kill him. You got it, Nina?" he yelled at her, threatening her as he stood up.

"Yes. Oh God, but what about you? What about Stacy and the others?"

His eyes widened and his expression changed to one of pure evil. She knew that look. It meant trouble. It meant whomever did him wrong was done.

He yanked the belt from the waist of his pants and ran it over his palm.

"My business is my business. Not yours!" he yelled and struck her over her shoulder.

"Please, Rico, don't. I don't understand."

"You will soon enough." He struck her again and again as he warned her that she was to keep quiet, to do as he said, and to never leave him. He said he could be with whomever he wanted to be with. That he could fuck one, two, three women together if he wanted to because he was the boss, the man.

Nina cried out and begged him to stop. She was petrified and then came the anger, the disgust knowing she had been had. It was a lie. All his words and his actions were lies.

"Please, Rico. I will obey. I'll obey," she told him as she continued to cry.

She wondered where things had gone so wrong. Who was this man, this monster, she adored and thought was her future, her destiny? She didn't know him and her need to feel loved had her making bad choices one after the other. She gave him her virginity and her heart, and he'd stomped on it like a bug.

Rico stopped, but her body continued to convulse in the aftereffects of his abuse and the extent of her emotional turmoil.

He fell to his knees and pulled her up by her cheeks. His dark, almost black eyes bore into hers.

"God, look what you made me do. Nina, you're special to me. So very special. You are my everything, but I have needs, desires that are too corrupt, evil, dirty for someone so sweet as you. You need to accept this. You are mine, Nina."

"But why another woman? If what you say is true, then why cheat on me? Why do you need to have sex with someone else? If you didn't want me anymore, you should just tell me so I can leave." The tears struck her eyes because she really didn't want that to be true. Life would be so difficult, so lonely without Rico or anyone she knew. All her friends were his friends. All her acquaintances were Rico's. She truly would have nothing, would be completely on her own, and it scared her more than his strikes and his disgust with her.

His eyes grew darker, his grip on her cheeks tightened and he clenched his teeth as he spoke softly, yet with such power.

"I don't think you understand. You're mine. No other man will ever have you. This is your life now. I say when it's over." He was silent and his words tore her heart open and made her realize how stupid she had been.

He shoved away from her with an expression of disgust, yet he was the one who struck her cheek, caused her to hit her head and bleed, and the one who caused the deep red marks across her shoulders, back, and arms.

"Tell me you love me, Nina."

Her lips were quivering. She was petrified. Why would he ask that now, when obviously he didn't love her?

He raised his hand at her.

"I love you," she said and cried out, the tears rolling down her cheeks.

"You need to show me. Get undressed, and get on the bed."

Her eyes widened in shock. The last thing she wanted right now was for him to have her. She obviously didn't move quickly enough as he pulled her up by her blouse, ripping the material and lifting her to her tiptoes.

His face was against hers, his spittle hitting her cheeks and eyes.

She could smell Stacy's cheap perfume. Could see the lipstick marks on his neck this close to him. She scrunched her eyes together and tried not to breathe her scent in. It was all consuming. The realization that this man she thought she loved didn't love her and now would degrade her in such a way caused turmoil and disgust to swirl in her empty belly. She felt this sudden hollow sensation, like she was going to die. Like even if he forced the sex on her tonight and she survived his abuse that she would lose what little bit of soul she had left.

Rico shook her. "You're going to learn the hard way. I'm in charge of you, Nina. You do as I say, or your punishments will be worse. Now get undressed or I'll do it for you."

She reached for the buttons, her fingers shaking. She didn't do it fast enough and he grabbed at her blouse, tearing it off of her. Her large breasts bounced. The red bra she wore under the black blouse had been meant for him but that was before. Before Stacy, before his abuse, and before he degraded her and let her know he used her for her virginity and innocence.

She stared at him in his dress pants, the belt in his other hand, his chest heaving, his red lips wet from his yelling. He was no longer the sexy, attractive man she had thought she loved. Instead she saw him as the monster he really was.

He struck her again and yelled for her to get undressed. His strike was so hard she turned and hit the side dresser. She grabbed onto the solid wood. In her mind she had flashbacks of years ago when she was a little girl and her mother brought home one of her johns. The man was drunk, abusive, and he struck her mother, grabbed her by her hair and dragged her to the bedroom. Her mom's eyes locked onto Nina's. That lost look was how Nina felt right now. After all she went through, was she going to turn into her mother, the woman who died in some alleyway with none of the men she gave her own daughter up for?

She locked gazes with the marble statue of a dolphin. The anger, the disgust and hatred, filled her belly. She was desperate to be free. Rico had so much power and control that Nina could never leave him or escape from this destiny, as he called it.

He struck her with the belt across her back and she felt her skin break. He hit her again and then ripped her skirt. He was going to rape her. Her mind scattered into a thousand directions and was lost in the past and where she had been and how she wound up here. Just like her mother. A woman used by one man and eventually others would take from her what they wanted, too. She had wanted a better life. She wanted to succeed, to make it and be someone. But just as women before her, she allowed a man to take control of her destiny and use her.

The repeated strikes to her back sent her over the edge as her skin felt as if it tore, and she cried out in anger.

She gripped the marble dolphin and used all her strength to pick up the thing and swung it around her.

She was shocked as she hit Rico just right. He fell to the ground, blood dripping from his skull, and passed out.

She was shaking as she dropped the marble dolphin on the floor, then slowly moved toward Rico. The man was not moving. She feared she'd killed him as she covered her mouth and cried out. She was shaking with anger, fear, and emptiness. It wasn't that she cared about him at all now. Not after what he did to her, degrading her, cheating on her, abusing her, and then getting ready to rape her. She realized she felt nothing. She had been living in a fantasy because she feared taking on life alone. Not anymore.

She wouldn't get too close to him. She feared him now more than anything else. She kicked his foot and nothing happened.

"Oh God, did I kill him?" she asked aloud to no one. She felt terrible and then reminded herself that he was going to hurt her badly. She felt the stinging pain on her back caused by him. The throbbing in her cheeks, her lips, and her entire body caused by Rico. She had no choice. This wasn't the same man she had fallen in love with.

It was a moment of realization, an epiphany. She could stay here, continue to be abused, neglected, used, and eventually wind up dead, or she could live. She could go out there and make something of her life, even temporary. She looked at Rico's body, around the apartment, then back at him.

She knew she couldn't leave him like this. Not dead and then run. She slowly knelt down on the rug and reached toward his neck. She felt his pulse. And he moaned.

She pulled back, jumped up, and frantically looked around the room. She didn't know what to do. She went over everything in her head and wondered if this would be her only opportunity to escape his grasp. He thought he owned her. He said it himself that she was his. He was going to continue to have sex with all these women and keep her as his woman, too. She had become a possession, an obsession for him and nothing more. He kept her because she never had sex with anyone but him. He was sick in the head. She would die if she stayed here.

She felt disgusted and angry. She needed to make a quick decision. Stay here and be a victim of this monster, be his whore, his piece of property or run, escape to a better life, a new life elsewhere, and far, far away from Rico.

The tears spilled from her eyes. Could she survive on her own, all alone? Or was she too weak, too dependent on Rico?

I'm all alone. I have no one.

She thought about calling the police, but knowing that Rico knew so many cops around here, this situation would get turned around on her. No, she had to run. She had to get the hell out of here and never look back.

He moaned again and she knew time was running out. If she stayed now, he'd probably kill her, and Rico knew people.

The decision was made and she ran to the closet, pulled out her bags, and started throwing everything into them. She knew she only had a little bit of money. Rico was going to be very angry and he could try to come after her. She went over to the dresser and pulled out his wallet. She took a wad of money from it and then went into dresser drawer and took more. Enough to get her across the state, and somewhere safe, small, where she could blend in and begin a new life. She could put Rico and this mess behind her. She could live instead of stay here and die.

She didn't count it. She just stuffed into her purse and looked around to see if she forgot anything. She didn't have time. She couldn't keep the mementos because this life was over.

She ran past him, heard his muffled moans getting louder. He was going to come to. Then she ran toward the dresser and took his phone and put it into the toilet bowl in the bathroom. Like many people he didn't memorize people's numbers. He had them locked in under their code. She was buying more time. He would call Cougar and Alex, his two best buddies and security. Perhaps even Martino and Miguel, the two thugs who hung around sometimes at the club who looked like murderers.

She shuddered just thinking about the two crazy men. Her body ached and burned, her cheek was incredibly sore, and she knew she should probably see a doctor but she couldn't now. She was on the run. She needed to get as far away from San Francisco as possible.

She ran toward the door, looked back one last time at her old life, and headed out the door, slamming it closed behind her.

I can do this. I can survive on my own without a man, without anyone, and live. I just want to live and not feel any more pain again.

Chapter 1

Six Months Later

Detective Buddy Landers was running late. He was supposed to meet his brothers, Trent and Johnny, plus Ace, Bull, and Ice at the Station for drinks. First, he took a phone call in his truck from another detective in regards to a domestic violence assault in Fairway, one town over. The woman was involved in a relationship with the guy for the past six months when he started becoming abusive. One night a week ago things got out of hand. The police were called, but the boyfriend resisted arrest. They took him in. He was released the next day when the girlfriend didn't press charges. Then three days later the girlfriend turned up dead. It was terrible. It seemed to Buddy that abuse was a vicious cycle. It was heartbreaking to think that this woman loved this guy so much she forgave him only for him to lose his cool again and kill her.

Buddy shook his head as the detective informed him that the boyfriend admitted to the murder. He fessed up to his attorney and said he didn't want to go through a long trial trying to pretend he wasn't guilty.

Buddy disconnected the call and headed inside when he heard his name.

"Buddy." He turned around even though he knew he recognized the voice. It was out of habit of being respectful and courteous, unlike the individual approaching.

Tara Kelly. A lying bitch who tried to press charges against his brother Johnny for sexual harassment. *The bitch has nerve calling my name and wanting to talk to me. She caused nothing but aggravation and a temporary suspension for Johnny until his innocence was proven. Which was within two weeks. What the fuck does she want with me?*

He crossed his arms in front of his chest and stood there in his protective stance. It was one he used when questioning criminals or trying to intimidate an untrustworthy person.

She flung her long blonde hair off her shoulder so she could show off her breasts. The woman's choice of dresses got shorter and shorter, tighter and tighter every time she came around.

"I thought that was you. How are you?" She smiled then winked. He kept his arms in place. He wasn't going to take a chance that this woman would say he tried something on her.

"I have nothing to say to you, Tara."

"You're not still angry with me about Johnny, are you? I mean, it was my mistake. I took his flirting the wrong way."

"Flirting the wrong way? You accused him of practically forcing himself on you. Sexual harassment is a very serious crime. It cost him his good reputation, a suspension on his record, never mind the social aspect of it."

"It all worked out. Is he here tonight? Is Trent here, too?" she asked, straining her neck to look past him and into the main room.

"Listen, you stay clear of my family, you got it? We don't like you. We don't have anything to say to you."

She reached out and touched his arm, but he pulled away.

"Don't touch me. Take a hike."

She looked him over. Those soft, sinful eyes looked at him with lust and then with evil intentions. He didn't trust the woman as far as he could throw her. He turned and walked away from her and toward his brothers. He saw Johnny's facial expression. The guy looked pissed off and worried. Tara's damn accusations caused them all relationship problems. Plus they were so untrusting of women that none of them had dated anyone for nearly six months.

Something had to give soon. Johnny needed to get over the sexual harassment thing. Most knew he was innocent. Trent needed to not be so concerned about a woman seeing the burns on his body from a fire a few years ago, and Buddy, he needed to stop taking his work home with him. Every case affected him. But mostly the ones where women were victims, or men were abusive to some really sweet women.

He couldn't help but to think that he and his brothers were good men. Compassionate, caring men who would never lay a hand on a woman or be controlling. Despite all the negatives of each of their individual relationship problems, Buddy and his brothers knew one thing for sure. They wanted to share a woman. They wanted one that could understand their individuality yet accept them as a package. Together. It wasn't so easy. They each had strong personalities and expected a lot from any woman they were with, even one-night stands. They were particular, and they were passionate.

But looking at Trent and Johnny, and feeling pretty damn lonely and unconfident they would find someone, he hoped that things would change soon. If they didn't, then each of them would fall deeper and deeper within themselves and never open up their heart again to another woman.

* * * *

"You guys are out of your minds. I can't believe that Serefina is letting the three of you hang out with us at the Station tonight," Buddy Landers said. His brothers, Trent and Johnny, chuckled.

"She's an amazing woman. If she were ours, we'd be home with her right now." Trent Landers teased his cousins some more.

"Yeah, right. You three are never going to settle down. Too caught up in your careers," Ace said then took a slug of beer.

"That's not it at all," Johnny added as he looked around the Station and then back toward his cousins.

"Who the hell do you keep looking around for?" Buddy asked his brother.

"No one. Just looking." Johnny winked at Bull before he took a slug of beer.

"You're all talk, Johnny," Trent told his brother and then looked at Ice.

"So, any new leads on those small fires in Fairway and near town?" Ice asked Trent, who was the arson investigator for the county. It included Treasure Town and Fairway, a town adjacent to theirs.

"So far no one has seen a soul around that seemed suspicious. I can tell you that they're amateur, though. There's nothing complicated or clever about their setups or accelerants."

"But they're getting brazen. My concern is how far they'll go for the attention they're starting to get with the media," Buddy added.

"Yeah, that's all we need is for this person or people to start hitting occupied buildings," Trent replied, looking angry.

"Oh no, we definitely don't want that. Have the neighborhood watch programs started yet or is the town board still holding up the process?" Bull asked.

"You know how they are over there in Fairway. They think the moment the signs go up that say 'Neighborhood Watch' the neighborhood will lose its upscale name. They fear people won't want to buy in the new condominiums going up along the causeway," Johnny Landers told them. They all agreed.

"Well, they should focus on how secure it will appear with those signs posted. To me it states that the townspeople are looking out for one another and aren't afraid to report crime if any occur. It's a good thing," Bull said.

"We have that here in Treasure Town. I just don't see what the big deal is," Ice said.

"I don't know either. I'm supposed to meet with Charles Walters from the board. I have our board here in Treasure Town making themselves available for any questions or concerns they might have so we can get things moving on the neighborhood watch. Buddy talked with the sheriff and Jake is on board with having a few extra patrols circling the area at night especially. That seems to be when our little arsonist is most busy," Trent said.

"Well, good. Spreading the word is important. But people also have to be aware of what's going on around their neighborhoods. This is their home and arson isn't something to take lightly," Ice said, and they all agreed.

"Well, wish me luck for tomorrow. This ought to be pretty darn interesting," Trent said. They chuckled, even though they were all concerned about stopping this criminal before things got out of hand.

* * * *

Once the guys left and it was just Trent, Buddy, and Johnny, Trent thought about what their cousins said. Trent and his brothers hadn't been serious in a relationship ever. They hadn't even met anyone lately that interested them. Trent had the hardest time being intimate with a woman. He tended to go for the no-strings-attached thing, and he knew why. He was self-conscious about the burns on his body. He went through a stage where he didn't feel good enough for a pretty woman. Especially with his brothers and him wanting to share. Finding someone who fit all their personalities and who they each found attractive was difficult.

"What's that expression for?" Buddy asked Trent. Johnny looked up, and although no words were exchanged, Trent felt as if Johnny's mind was on the same thing.

"I was just thinking about the prospects here tonight," he lied and glanced around the bar. It was the same people. He even noticed a few women he'd hooked up with over the last year. His stomach churned. Neither were relationship material and as pompous and as much of a double standard that it was, he didn't want to settle down with leftovers. Those women probably slept with plenty of men over the years. He was getting older, pickier about women, and he was feeling like settling down wasn't going to happen.

"There's nothing different, nothing that snags my attention. Besides, aren't you guys getting tired of this shit?" Buddy asked, and then took a slug of beer from the bottle he held.

"Don't start, Buddy," Trent ordered.

Buddy sat forward, looked around then at Johnny and back toward Trent.

"Why the fuck not? If we are serious about settling down and putting the single life behind us, then we need to be on the same page while we're looking."

"You don't set out looking for a partner, a wife. It will lead to trouble and heartache. There may not be anyone out there who's right for the three of us. Just accept it, Buddy. I have," Trent said.

"I disagree. I think she's out there and we just need to keep our eyes open."

"Johnny, you're a dreamer. Listen to your oldest brother. I've got years on you, kid. Women come and women go. They can use guys just like guys use women. Don't go falling for any traps. You're feeling horny, go over to see Jessica. She'll take you home and make you a happy man for the night and not even expect a call or even an acknowledgment afterward."

"Fuck, Trent, why do you have to be such a coldhearted asshole sometimes? I mean, what the fuck," Johnny said loudly and ran his hand through his hair before banging his fist on the table.

"Trent, he's right. What's your problem?" Buddy asked.

"Me? I don't have a problem. I get it, that's all." He refused to get into a deep conversation with them on the subject.

"Trent, it's okay to be self-conscious about—"

"Shut the fuck up, Buddy. Don't. I'm not fucking having this conversation with you. Just order another round or we'll head out. It's over."

Trent looked away from his brothers with a heavy heart and an emptiness that reached his gut. He wanted what his cousins had, what their friends had. He, Johnny, and Buddy wanted to be in a serious relationship with a wonderful woman and share her, take care of her, make her a real part of them. They wanted a family, a completion in their lives. But with all their individual heavy baggage, it wasn't looking achievable. Every woman they met so far didn't give them the sensations they knew were necessary for a committed relationship. He couldn't help but wonder if their woman, the right woman, was even out there for them.

I'm thirty-four years old, a workaholic, and will probably end up alone. No beautiful, perfect woman is going to want such an imperfect bastard like me. Scars and all. Fuck it.

Trent got up while Buddy and Johnny were still trying to talk to him and he walked out of the Station. He just couldn't bear the feelings of inadequacy. Not tonight. Not every night of his life.

Chapter 2

"This whole place smells incredible. Where the heck did you learn how to bake like that, Nina?" Cindy asked.

Nina smiled. She had gotten her first order for three apple pies for a party Cindy's parents were throwing. Nina had handed out a bunch of fliers and was planning on baking a dozen or so pies and giving out samples to a few of the restaurants and cafés on and near the boardwalk. She was so nervous because this apartment she was renting was super small. The oven was shit, but she just needed to watch it carefully to not burn her crusts.

"I'm self-taught, and I love it. I really would enjoy owning my own little bakery someday, but I need to get my pies out there first."

"Honey, if your apple pies taste as delicious as the one you baked for my parents to sample, you'll be getting orders in no time."

Nina smiled as she went about making the pies.

She looked at Cindy, who was texting some guy she liked. Cindy wanted Nina to go out, but Nina wasn't ready for that. Her focus was on making some money, establishing a following for her pies so she could start a small business. It wasn't going to be easy, especially as she tried to hide her past, her real last name, and work without proper identification. She should have remembered to grab her driver's license. But then again she didn't own a car, couldn't afford one anyway, and if she used her ID anywhere where it was processed through a computer, then Rico could find her.

She swallowed that sick sensation she felt instantly as she thought of Rico.

Thank goodness she met Fannie. She was working for Fannie Higgins, a nice lady who offered her a part-time job at her little boutique called Angel's Wings.

It had been six months since she left California with only two bags of clothing and three thousand dollars. She was very careful about how she spent the money, using more to sleep in a motel instead of on the streets somewhere if the neighborhoods seemed worse than others. She was grateful to be in the small apartment despite it being above a liquor store.

She remembered finding this place. Treasure Town. Even the name had a mystical appeal laced with new beginnings and fantasies come true. She wanted her happy ever after, goddamn it! She giggled to herself. What was she thinking? She was a realist now. Cynical even to a fault, after what life threw at her. Her inability to trust held her back from sharing anything about herself or her past. When she thought about Rico, she shook with fear. She didn't need the added stress. Her evenings in bed filled with nightmares, panic attacks, and cold sweats were enough anxiety to live with.

"So, are you working at Fannie's tomorrow?"

"Yes. She's trying to give me some more hours, but the store really runs itself. People browse around looking, reading all the spiritual sayings and things. You really can't bother them or ask to assist them."

"I didn't think of that. Are you still looking for other work? I can ask Florence if she needs another waitress at Sullivan's."

"I'll let you know. Maybe she needs some fresh-baked pies to sell there?"

"I can ask her. They order in from the city and get deliveries. But it would be great to advertise a local girl's homemade pies." Cindy smiled and winked.

Nina placed the last two pies onto the counter.

"I'm not a local girl, remember? But I like the concept."

"Who cares that you weren't born here. You live here now. Your pies are 'delish,' and you're gorgeous. What more could make someone stand up and notice you?"

"I don't know, but if you think of anything, let me know please. I'm getting desperate. Oh, and I'm not gorgeous." She shyly looked down and wiped her flower-sprinkled hands on her apron. She didn't like to receive that kind of attention from anyone. She knew her eyes stood out more than most. It was her one asset that she was blessed with. People had referred to them as spirited eyes, magical, entrancing, and some other words she really didn't bother to overthink.

"You really don't think you're beautiful, do you, Nina?" Cindy asked as she put her phone away, stood up straight, and placed her hands on her hips.

"I know we haven't known one another long at all, but girl, your eyes alone are a knockout. I mean, I've never seen such mocha-colored eyes, and they practically glow around the edges. You have that olive complexion, the whole Italian–Sicilian thing going on, and your body? I think I'm going to take up walking. Cause your form of transportation has you sporting a killer ass and toned thighs, too. You're gorgeous, woman. Don't ever let anyone ever tell you otherwise," Cindy told her.

Nina was shocked at Cindy's description of her. She didn't like to think of herself as beautiful. Especially with the faint scars along her forearms and the ones on her ass. Rico really hit her hard with his belt that day. If she hadn't been on the run for so long, she would have used some money to get some ointment to prevent scarring. But that wasn't the case. She was on the run, and he was going to hunt her down unless she disappeared.

"Hey, what's that look for?" Cindy asked, touching her hand. When she did, Nina immediately pulled away. She tried to step around the small space but Cindy stopped her.

"Nina, I know we haven't known one another long, but I care about you. You're a lot like I was a few years back. Living on my own, no family, trying to make ends meet and get through this life. But sometimes you just have this far-off look, and I can't help to think that you're afraid of something. I don't know what it is. I know your life and your past is none of my business. Hell, I guess what I'm trying to say is that if you need a friend, I'm here for you."

Nina felt her chest tighten. How much she wanted to accept that friendship and admit some of her fears to Cindy but she couldn't. It was easier, wiser, she knew from experience, to just stay hollow inside and alone.

"I appreciate that. I've never had a close friend before. Thanks." She turned around and placed the pies into a large cardboard box. She placed three apple pies into another box for Cindy.

"So let me know what your mom and her friends think, okay?"

"Will do." Cindy closed her eyes and inhaled.

"If these pies make it to the house. Damn, girl, these smell so good." Nina smiled at the compliment and then opened the door for Cindy, who headed out.

As Nina closed the door, she leaned back against it, feeling that tightness in her chest.

Will I ever be able to have a friend? Will I ever feel strong enough and safe enough to get close to anyone? God, life is going to be lonely. All I have is my baking abilities. Please God. Please let these people love my pies and place some orders. Please.

Chapter 3

"That answer isn't good enough, Alex. Nina has been gone for six months, six fucking months. How the hell could she be surviving out there on her own without me?"

"I don't know, Rico. Obviously she's more capable and resourceful than we all gave her credit for," he replied.

"Bullshit!" Rico slammed his fist down on the table. He stared at Cougar.

"What's your take on this? Any leads at all?"

Cougar shook his head. "None. She's gone, Rico. Can't you just forget about her? You have a dozen others who can replace her," Alex added.

Rico stared at him and then stared at the picture of Nina on his desk.

Her eyes were a shade of mocha so incredible that it was as if they glowed around the edges. She was submissive, controllable, until he pushed too hard, too far.

"She is too special. She is perfect, and I pushed her to the edge."

"How can you say that? You gave her so much. You got what you wanted from her, her innocence, her virginity," Cougar countered.

Rico shot a look at him. "It was more than that. By taking her first, by possessing her fully, she became mine. No one takes what is mine. She belongs to me and always will. I will stop at nothing to find her. Do you hear me, Alex? I will stop at nothing. I want more people on this. When we have her back, things will change. The club is running itself. Cougar, you could stay on as manager while I take Nina away for a while. You know, to get her used to her permanent position by my side. I will teach her to obey me, and do whatever I ask of her."

"And what about what Martino and his brother Miguel want?" Cougar asked. "They were waiting on you to share her with them and that was supposed to happen the night she took off."

Rico bit the inside of his cheek. "I said I wouldn't share her despite the proposition they offered."

"They offered a great deal, a partnership across the Caribbean. Is she really worth all this? Is it worth it to make her return to appease your obsession, only for you to be forced to share her with Miguel and Martino?" Cougar asked.

Rico stared at Cougar. He had been with him for the last seven years. He was more than just his head of security and guard. He was family.

"I need to do what I must. I'll face that decision of sharing her when the time comes. All I ask of you two right now is to keep digging. She's out there. She's alive, and I will not stop looking until I find her and have her in my arms. I'll never give up looking. Never."

* * * *

Nina was feeling a bit frustrated from not receiving any orders after Cindy's mom's party the other day. Fannie Higgins let her place flyers on the counter by the register at Angel's Wings, but no bites yet.

She was using Cindy's cell phone number and e-mail because she couldn't afford a phone for herself, nor was she willing to risk setting up an e-mail account, giving Rico a way to track her down.

The store was quiet today, and it was getting close to closing time as Nina picked up one of the little cards on the rack that caught her eye. It had a picture of a small blueberry pie at the top. "Life is as sweet as the ingredients you put into it. A dash of spice, a little bit of sugar, a lot of love, and sweet results."

She chuckled and then placed the card back down. The store was filled with so many cool things and not all the sayings were spiritual. Some were just intuitive and witty phrases.

There were all different sections catering to all emotions and life events. There were cards suitable to give someone in mourning, congratulations, best wishes, get well soon, inspiration. She walked over to the wind chimes that appeared so mystical and sounded pretty. They had some seashells and other little things that she loved to hear when they connected and chimed. If she had a house with a front porch, she'd buy one. But right now her cramped one-bedroom apartment above the small liquor store was not exactly home. It was hers for now and what she could afford for the next few months. Then it might be back to the parks and other areas where it was safe to sleep outdoors. She swallowed hard.

"You could get going, Nina. I don't expect many more customers in the last twenty minutes," Fannie said.

"Are you sure? Do you need anything else done?" she asked, heading back toward the counter.

"Nope, we're good. I'll see you in a couple of days."

"Yes, ma'am," Nina said and took her purse from behind the counter.

"Be careful walking, there are some crazy drivers around here at night."

"I will. Thank you," Nina said and headed outside. The air was still nice and warm. The sun had set already and darkness began to overtake the town. She walked past the sign that said "Welcome to Treasure Town" on her way toward the apartment. It wasn't far from here at all.

As she rounded the corner, noticing a few people walking and holding hands or heading toward the beach for a night walk, she caught sight of a flicker of red and orange. Someone was lighting a match or something, and they looked to be a teenager.

She figured they were lighting a cigarette so she continued walking. As she got closer, she noticed the blond hair that stuck out from the Yankee's baseball hat he wore, and then she saw his face.

He was a nice-looking kid, but his expression immediately changed to anger as he abruptly turned away. Her gut clenched as she made her way down the sidewalk, never looking back at him again. She also noticed the red jersey he wore with the word "Costa" on the back. At least that was what she thought it said.

The liquor store was still open and busy. But as she headed toward the door, she looked around to be sure no drunks were hiding anywhere then unlocked it and walked upstairs to her apartment. She hated always having this fearful, on-edge feeling in her gut. She was never at ease, never feeling safe or calm at all. She was getting tired of it. Something had to give.

She couldn't help but think about the kid's jersey. Maybe it was a school name. She never had the opportunity to go to college but she did finish high school. Of course she was never part of a team, never wore the colors or the mascot of the black cougar on her shirt. She couldn't afford anything even if she wanted to. But at least she got her diploma. When she thought about the cougar on the shirt, she thought about Rico's right hand man. Cougar was a maniac. He thought nothing of rearranging someone's face just for looking at him, Rico, or even her the wrong way.

Thank God Cougar wasn't at the apartment that night she was attacked. She never would have escaped. She'd be either hospitalized or dead.

She swallowed hard and grabbed a bottle of water from the refrigerator. The place was very warm tonight and stuffy. There was no air-conditioning. The apartments with those cost a bit more a month. She reached for a hair band and pulled her long brown locks into a makeshift pony and added the hair band. Pulling her hair higher on her head the few seconds of relief from the heat off her neck didn't last long. She headed toward the window, pushed it open, and looked out across the streets and at all the little beat-up storefronts. At least five or six blocks up were the homes and apartments closest to the beach. Maybe one day she would live someplace closer.

The thought sobered her good mood and made her think about her current financial situation. She either needed to land some baking jobs this week or she was going to have to put that on hold and venture out into the social world and get a job waitressing. That meant talking to people, mingling, and making conversation. She sucked at that. She was shy, liked keeping to herself. There had to be something else she could do for money.

She took a deep breath and released it.

Tomorrow she would bring the pies by the restaurants on the boardwalk and try to sell them or at minimum get the owners to taste test them. Maybe Cindy was successful with Sullivan's? She would find out soon enough, or it was going to be back on the streets for her, and no semisoft bed to lay her head on at night.

* * * *

Trent Landers was starving as he stopped by the boardwalk in between questioning a witness a few blocks over and heading back to the department for more paperwork and research. He decided on a slice of pizza and wanted to sit at one of the shaded tables that looked out toward the water. He loved living in Treasure Town. It had so much to offer and was growing in leaps and bounds. The department was expanding and Jake McCurran, the sheriff, was looking into hiring more deputies. The board meeting on the budget was in a few weeks.

It sure was hot out today, and the beaches were crowded, the boardwalk, too. It kind of made him think about the off-season when the tourists weren't around and the people walking or frequenting the boardwalk were locals. It was a hell of a lot less crowded and quieter, too.

He enjoyed the peacefulness of sitting on the beach and listening to the tide role in. It would be even better if there were a woman by his side along with his brothers sharing it.

With thoughts of sharing a sunset with a woman and his brothers, came thoughts of sharing a woman period. The idea was pounding in his brain lately, thanks to Buddy and Johnny.

Maybe he just needed to get laid? Perhaps that would ease this constant ache inside his heart. But with that thought came the feelings of inadequacy and imperfection. He ignored those thoughts and looked around at the people when his eyes landed on something special. Something clicked. Something inside of him, like a radar, clicked on and all he could do was stare. Thank God he wore his dark sunglasses.

How pretty. She's beautiful.

* * * *

Nina was hungry. She was feeling a little light headed and knew she better go for eating a little breakfast. She could skip lunch, and probably swing a slice of pizza for dinner. Having three meals a day just wasn't realistic. Not without income coming in. Before she left the apartment, she had a couple of hundred bucks left.

She walked past the various venders. Everything looked so good, but as she read the menu price boards, she cringed. Eight dollars for a small sausage-and-pepper sandwich? There wasn't even a drink with it or a side?

She bypassed that and continued walking, feeling more and more light headed.

She opted for the pizza place, and as she stood in the heat behind a couple of guys, she could see the homemade lemonade station. Glancing at the price, she knew she could afford the slice and the drink. With lots of ice. It was hot out here today.

When it was her turn to order, she told the kid what she wanted and asked for the lemonade while she waited for the slice. Maybe a little sugar would help her? She took a sip and glanced around. Her eyes locked onto a big guy in dress pants and a button-down shirt. But what really stood out aside from his good looks and dark expression were the gun and badge.

She quickly turned away, the motion nearly causing her to lose her balance. She grabbed onto the counter ledge.

"You okay, honey?" some guy asked as he eyed her over. She knew that look. He couldn't be trusted. He was looking to take advantage of her. Her slice was up. She grabbed it and her lemonade and looked around for a table to sit at. The one in the shade was where the cop was. She felt so fearful and like a criminal who was wanted and on the run. This guy was really intimidating and looked older than her by at least five or so years. She wasn't certain.

"Are you okay?" he asked her. She didn't want to sit there, to join him and make him think that she was flirting, but the truth was that she needed food and she needed to sit before she passed out. This running around looking for work and trying to sell her pies on one meal a day was weighing on her.

She plopped down, very unladylike, into the seat. She held her head, but didn't look up at the guy. "Thanks. It's hot."

"Take a sip of the lemonade before you pass out," he ordered.

She snapped her head up to look at him. She didn't know why but she was half-scared and half-confused by his tone. The man was tall, even sitting down, and as he stared at her, trying to read her mind, she locked gazes with his blue eyes.

"I'll be okay. Just eating lunch a little late." She glanced away to take a sip of lemonade. Then she set the cup down and lifted up the slice of pizza. It was delicious and the cheese gooey. As she pulled the slice away, the cheese hit her chin.

She quickly set the slice down and reached for a napkin.

"You're not from around here are you?" he asked and her belly tightened. She shook her head and then took another bite of the pizza.

"New in town or just passing through?" he asked. *Shit. Why the hell is he asking me questions? Do I look guilty of something? Shit, what do I do?*

"I'm thinking about sticking around, and you? Are you a cop or something?" she asked, turning the conversation around.

"Arson investigator," he replied, still holding her gaze.

"But you have a gun."

He widened his eyes. "Yeah, well they give those out to anyone who has a badge."

She realized he was teasing and she smiled softly then went back to eating.

* * * *

Trent Landers was in shock. He didn't quite recognize the sensations going through his body as he first caught site of the pretty little brunette. She seemed like she didn't feel well or might faint from the heat, but she was keeping it together. He couldn't believe he told her, ordered her, to sit down at his table. How fucking rude. But she did it, and it aroused him, made him feel like she respected him and took him seriously.

But as he found himself asking her questions, he couldn't help but wonder who she was, if she were single and lived around here, and how he could get to know her better. He needed to feel her out. The more questions he asked, the more nervous and unresponsive she became. He couldn't help but wonder if she was up to something. She ate the pizza in no time, basically gobbled it down, and now sipped from the lemonade container.

"Do you live near the boardwalk?" he asked her. She looked at him sideways.

"I'm sorry, I don't mean to be rude, but I don't know you."

He couldn't help but to stare at her. Her eyes were mesmerizing, just like the rest of her. She was very attractive and young. He felt this tingling in his chest. He identified it as concern maybe because she had looked like she might pass out. He didn't want to just walk away, but he didn't want her to think he was some pervert.

"Sorry. Force of habit. I'll leave you to your lunch," he said, even though she'd chowed it down already. She must have been starving. She looked thin, but still shapely. Why did he think for a moment she was hiding something?

He got up was about to walk away when he noticed the look of relief on her face. She *was* up to something. What the hell was it and why did he even care?

He walked away but didn't head back to his truck, instead he mingled through the crowds and kept an eye on her. He told himself it was because he was concerned. He wouldn't want a young, attractive woman like her to pass out from heat exhaustion and have some random guy come to her aid. Again he had that tightness in his chest. Why would he care if some random guy got to touch her, hold her in his arms?

He cursed under his breath and continued to watch her. Should he go back and flirt? Maybe try to get her number?

Instantly the idea of someone as beautiful and sweet as her seeing his scars caused a numbing sensation to expand over his body and make certain parts deflate, including his ego.

"Forget her and walk away," he whispered.

* * * *

Nina stood by the railing and watched all the good-looking men enter the restaurant and café called Sullivan's. Cindy wasn't kidding when she said some of the best-looking first responders hung out there after their late shifts or even during the day. She should have gotten a clue after seeing that attractive older arson guy at the table near the pizza place. That guy was intense and attractive in such a way that she felt a little funny. Well, maybe not funny, but intrigued. Thinking about liking another man or even admitting to feeling attracted to someone felt scary. It was something she'd rather avoid entirely simply for the reason she could never act upon her emotions. Her poor judgment, lack of self-esteem, and desperate need to feel like she belonged had caused her to nearly die. Nina just wasn't willing to test fate one more time. She shoved those thoughts aside. She couldn't, wouldn't ever trust a man again. Not if her life depended on it.

Nina swallowed hard as she gripped the box with the six different pies in it. She hoped that Cindy wasn't lying about her boss wanting to meet Nina and try a piece of pie. She was shy, and she knew she needed to be a bit more outgoing, salesy yet friendly, and that made the nauseous feeling hit her gut.

Please don't let me puke.

She saw Cindy walk out the front door and wave her over. Nina's heart was pounding inside of her chest. She felt the lump in her now totally dry throat. Taking a deep breath, feeling her sweaty palms nearly lose her grip on the box, she took another deep breath, then another, and headed over.

The moment she entered the place all eyes fell upon her and she nearly lost her ability to walk. *Hol. Ly. Shit.*

Never in her life had she seen such attractive men all in one place. The male population definitely dominated in Treasure Town. Maybe that was the meaning behind the name. Because any woman lucky enough to snag one or more of these men had totally hit the jackpot.

Cindy helped her with the box. "Relax, they're just a bunch of regulars, and like I said, you're gorgeous. I just can't believe you're so oblivious to it." She chuckled then pulled her along. "This is your chance to sell your product. Good luck."

"Florence, this is Nina. Nina, meet my boss and one of the owners of Sullivan's." Cindy introduced them.

"Hello, Nina. I've been hearing an awful lot about your delicious pies. We usually order from a distributor out of town, but Cindy was insistent that we try your homemade pies."

"Oh, I understand," Nina began to say and Cindy gave her a nudge.

"Ain't nothing like a locally homemade pie though, Florence. Nina lives in town, just a few blocks over, and can make just about any pie you like," Cindy pushed.

Florence leaned forward and inhaled near the box. "God, these smell incredible. Is that cherry pie, too?"

"Yes, ma'am. I use all fresh ingredients from the farmers market around the corner, and I get my eggs fresh from them, too."

"Well, they look beautiful," Florence said and then looked up as someone approached.

"Whatcha got in there that smells so good?" the man asked. Florence chuckled.

"Nina, meet Lester. He works at the coffee bar here. And he just happens to be a connoisseur of pies. He does the ordering for the desserts," she said.

Nina smiled. "Hi, Lester. Would you like to try a piece? Your choice," she offered. His eyes lit up.

He rubbed his hands together. "Okay. I'll try the cherry pie. It looks as sweet as you, doll." He winked. She felt her cheeks warm and that tightness hit her chest, but she remained smiling.

Nina lifted the large cherry pie out of the box and then Cindy took out the others, placing them onto the counter. Lester cut into the pie, taking a small slice. He eyed over the slice as if he truly was an expert.

"These are fresh cherries? You soak them and all?"

"Yes, sir. My own recipe," she added.

"Hey, big guy, where's your whipped cream?" another man asked as he joined them and wrapped his arm around Florence's waist.

"This is my husband, Al. Al meet Nina. She baked all these pies herself. She's looking for us to order some to sell here."

"We order through the distributor."

"Oh, but these are homemade locally. You can't beat that, sir," Nina added confidently, even shocking herself as she felt her cheeks warm. She looked away, and then when she glanced back at Al, his lip curled up in a small smile. He watched her as if he were analyzing her and she felt that intimidated feeling again.

Please don't let me get sick in front of these people. Please let them love the pies and order from me. God, I need the money. I need to make it here or I'll have to leave and live on the streets. God, I don't want to do that again. It's so scary.

"Oh my God, this is delicious. I mean, not like just really good, fantastic." Lester used his fork to scrape up every bit of pie. Florence chuckled.

"Thank you, Lester," Nina said.

"Let me try," Al added and picked up and fork and dug into the pie on the side. Behind them Cindy was asking if they were buying the pies because a group of men smelled them and asked for one whole apple pie.

"My God, this is heaven. You made this yourself?" Al asked Nina. She felt her heart racing. She wanted to scream with joy that they loved her pies, but she knew that her luck couldn't be this good. Something was going to go wrong.

"How much do you want per pie this size, Nina?" Lester asked her.

She looked at Cindy. Shoot, she never thought about a price.

"Well, they are homemade, I do get all the fresh fruits from the market," she started to say.

"How about this. I get the pies, this size from the distributor for fifteen. If you can offer the same deal then I'll place an order with you and see how our customers respond? How does that sound?"

"That's a deal, Lester. Thank you so much." She reached out and shook his hand.

"Wonderful. How many pies are you going to need and what kind?" Cindy asked, handing Nina a pen and paper. Thank God because Nina was so shocked she thought she might pass out.

Lester rambled off the pies he wanted, and Florence smiled.

"So how about we take these for now, minus Lester's cherry pie," she teased as Lester held the rest of the pie pan in his hand as if he wouldn't let anyone else try some.

"The cherry pie is on me. It was a sample to let you see what you were buying," Nina told them.

"Excellent," she replied.

"Oh, I think we owe you for the others, too," Florence said.

"What others?" Al asked.

Nina looked on the counter and the pies were gone.

Cindy handed over some money.

"They paid twenty dollars a pie when I told them they were the last ones," Cindy said. Lester, Florence, and Al chuckled, but Nina felt her jaw drop.

"Twenty each?" she asked Cindy with tears in her eyes.

She was so thrilled. If this kept up, she would be able to save some money and rent a bigger place with a better oven sooner than later.

"A hundred bucks for five pies, and about a dozen very satisfied firefighters with sweet teeth," Cindy teased.

Nina felt the tears reach her eyes. "Thank you, Cindy," she said and then turned toward Florence, Al, and Lester.

"Thank you so much for this opportunity. I won't let you down."

"You'd better not. I expect eight more pies here tomorrow morning by eight. Can you handle that?" Lester asked.

"Yes, sir. Thank you."

"No, thank you, Nina. We're so glad that Cindy told us about you and your homemade pies. Before long the other restaurants will be ordering, too," Al said.

"Maybe Nina's pies can be an exclusive here at Sullivan's?" Cindy suggested.

"Maybe?" Florence said.

"We'll talk about that after we see the response by her customers tomorrow."

"I'll be here by eight. Don't you worry," Nina exclaimed then shook their hands and headed out of the restaurant with money in her pocket and an empty box to fill with her supplies. If she hurried, she could still get some good product from the farmers market for the pies she had to make.

She was ecstatic as she headed down the boardwalk. She felt so positive about her life and about baking the best pies she could that she hurried back toward her apartment and the farmers market as fast as she could.

* * * *

Johnny was driving in the ambulance along with fellow paramedic Mercury St. James. They had finished up a call to the boardwalk where an older woman had heat stroke and seemed to be having chest pains. They took care of her, hooked her up to a heart monitor, took her vitals, and decided that she needed to go to the hospital as a precaution. Now they were back at it again. It was going to be a long night.

"Saw you guys all at the Station the other night. That crazy bitch Tara was hitting on Jenks. She had her hand down his pants at the table."

Johnny felt that instant anger at just hearing Tara's name. He had been stupid, had let his dick make a bad choice in character judgment. She had created the entire façade at the bar, pretending she slipped and fell and hurt her ankle. He still didn't know how she knew he was working and in the area. There were four other paramedics working the night shift. Or maybe she just got lucky that he showed up. She did seem thrilled with him immediately.

He was used to women flirting, especially when he responded to some incident they were involved in. Many claimed injuries that weren't real just to have him check them over.

If he was at all honest with himself, he'd admit that the power, the ability to do that, went to his head. Well, both heads.

"I don't even give a shit. I don't want to hear anything about her. Just tell me that Jenks didn't fall for her shit."

"He didn't. He fucked around with her and gave her a piece of her own medicine. She wasn't too happy about it or how she looked so easy. It was a crazy situation and her friends pulled her away when she started yelling at Jenks and the guys, then claiming she would get revenge."

"Oh shit, they better watch their asses. I wouldn't be surprised if they all have yellow sheets on their lockers this week."

"She wouldn't dare claim sexual harassment again. Not after she tried that with you and failed."

"She didn't fail, Mercury. I was out of work for two weeks, it's on my permanent record, and people who I thought knew me gave me shit. It was so fucked up. I still think some people believe I touched her sexually without her permission."

"Bullshit. If there is anyone who believes that, then they weren't your friend to begin with and they definitely don't know you and your brothers. No sweat, man. I just thought I would tell you what went down. If she's not careful, someone is going to really hurt her."

"That's not our problem. I just wish I could get over the whole situation. Seems to me that every time a woman flirts with me on a call, I step back and take extra precautions to make sure I don't touch her in any way that can be misconstrued at harassment."

"Damn, that's a shame. Because we get some pretty hot chicks sometimes and they're wearing hardly any clothing, and it's our job to be compassionate." Mercury raised his eyebrows up and down in a silly way.

"You're such an ass."

Mercury chuckled. "Just saying that there are perks to this job, and hot chicks flirting with us paramedics is pretty fucking great. I've been working out even more to keep in tip-top shape and try to get my arms looking like yours."

Johnny looked at his arms and then chuckled. "You need to work harder, dude. There's room on those sleeves."

Mercury scrunched his eyebrows together and appeared insulted. "Fuck. And I was thinking the shirt was getting tighter. Are you sure I don't look bigger?"

Johnny chuckled as he looked out the window while they drove down Luana Highway. "Maybe you should wear a shirt one size smaller. Then you'll look bigger."

Mercury shook his head. "Fuck you."

Johnny chuckled aloud.

But as they continued to drive around, waiting for their next call, he couldn't help but to think about where he was at and his true fear of trusting a woman. When something like this, a sexual harassment charge, was placed on a man with no grounds whatsoever, it changed him. Johnny changed a lot. He trusted less people. He overanalyzed women and their response to him. He wondered if he would ever get over his fear and actually even feel attracted to another woman again, and he didn't feel confident that his brothers would get over their fears, either.

Hell, their hope of finding a woman to share just like their cousins Ace, Ice, and Bull did was seeming more like a fantasy dream than something that could ever be a reality.

Life sucked, but this hollow feeling inside needed go. Johnny just didn't feel good about his life or himself with the weight on his heart and feelings of loneliness deep in his soul.

God, something's gotta give. Get rid of this feeling I have. Help me and my brothers, please.

* * * *

Nina was exhausted as she finished the last pie and placed them all into boxes, ready to be delivered to Sullivan's tomorrow morning. She sat on the window sill and let the light, not-so-cool breeze filter through the window. The apartment was extra hot with the oven on for so many hours but she was just grateful it didn't break. That was all she needed. Night had set in. With a quick glance at the clock, she could tell it was after midnight. She looked down at the street corner and noticed something, or someone, standing there.

She walked back over toward the living room and turned off the light. Then she walked back toward the window and thought she saw that kid again, the blond with the red jersey. He had a box or something and pushed it behind the Dumpster. Maybe it was garbage? Maybe he lived nearby and decided to place his garbage in the Dumpster? She wasn't sure, and honestly, she was too tired to care. She dragged herself to the bathroom and turned on the shower.

When she was finished, she threw on her lightest outfit, a tank and short shorts. With only four outfits to her name, making some money would help her wardrobe and her appearance. She really needed this job. It was bedtime and then the most important delivery of her life was at 8:00 a.m.

Please don't let this get all fucked up. Please let them love the pies, and like me.

* * * *

The sirens blared and the engines blew loudly as the fire trucks from Engine 19 approached the intersection along Luana Highway and four blocks away on Wilton Avenue. It was 1:00 a.m.

"We got a fire in the old liquor store. Looks like it started in the Dumpster on the right side," Ace Sullivan called out to his team of firefighters as they approached along with Engine 20.

The trucks pulled onto the scene and Eddie called out to Ace.

"There's an apartment on the top floor." He pointed out just as the paramedics arrived along with a deputy vehicle.

Ace, Eddie, Lance, and Bull climbed out of the truck and joined Engine 20, Chief Sanchez's team, as they approached.

"We got a call that someone smelled gas coming from the adjacent building. My team, Engine 20 will handle that if you guys from Engine 19 want to handle the fire," Sanchez said. Chief Martelli nodded.

He walked over to the men. "We got a possible gas leak next door. Not sure if it's related to this fire. I want to be sure that you're safe before you go in there."

"There's a young woman in that apartment on the top floor. She didn't come down. I think she's trapped," the owner of the liquor store called to them. Ace gave the orders and they prepared to head inside. On the hose were Bull and Eddie. John and Marcus Towers and Lance were working on getting the fire hydrants up and running. With all the flammable liquor beginning to pop and blast, it was becoming dangerous.

"We should head up the side staircase. There's a fire escape on the side. See it there?" Ace called out and just then they saw the woman, shorts, tank top, hair blowing around. She was carrying a big box out the window.

"What the hell is she doing?" Ace yelled out. They rushed to get to her as fire shot from the windows.

* * * *

Nina couldn't believe this was happening to her. She worked so hard to get these pie orders. She had been exhausted, had just gone to bed after taking her shower when the sound of sirens woke her. Then she smelled smoke. A sick feeling hit her gut as she realized she was about to lose everything, including the pies she baked for Sullivan's. She wasn't about to let some stupid fire ruin it all.

The heat of the flames was so intense she dropped the box. It was difficult to move quickly and not shake the pies and destroy them. She had to keep them in one piece. Just as she thought that, she heard the firefighters yelling. She felt the fire escape shaking and then a blast shot up from the bottom floor. Nina grabbed onto the metal as the entire fire escape tilted and sway, causing her box of pies to tumble to the ground below. She cried out in anger but then in pain as one of the pieces of metal scratched her side, cutting her. In a flash there were more firefighters yelling to her to hold on. She had no other choice. It was that or die.

Below she could see the numerous emergency vehicles arriving. The firefighter shoved a ladder against the wall right beside where she was. She swung her legs to the right, trying to reach it as a firefighter began climbing up.

"Hold on and I'll help you."

She wasn't about to trust some guy in a mask she didn't know. Nina grabbed onto the ladder, clung to it like some trained circus performer and began to make her way down. When the gloved hand went over her hips she remembered she wasn't exactly wearing a lot of clothing. Her side where the metal cut her skin was stinging, she was coughing from inhaling the smoke, and dried tears clung against her cheeks.

"I've got you, honey. Easy now," the firefighter said. As they got to the bottom, there were multiple firemen standing there and some paramedics.

"Bring her over here, Bull. Lay her on the gurney and we'll check her over," she heard someone say.

"I'm fine. I don't need to lie down," she said, fearful that they would maybe try to bring her to the hospital. That was a bill she couldn't pay and especially now that she lost all the pies and the money she had stashed under the mattress of the bed. But more importantly, she feared Rico finding her, and she wasn't about to make it easy for him by ending up in a computer system of a local hospital. She pulled from the paramedic and sat on the edge of the fire truck. She looked up toward the building lost in thought, her heart aching again at the sudden loss just when things were looking up.

"Sweetie, we need to check you out." The soothing voice and gentle touch drew back her attention to the present. As she turned to look at who was talking to her, her heart racing, her chest tight and about to release a deep cry, she locked gazes with a god. The man was absolutely gorgeous with big blue eyes, large muscles, and a sweet smile. He was a paramedic, dressed in navy blue, which made his tan complexion stand out even more. His blue eyes were so bold. She swallowed hard.

"Hey, are you okay?"

She nodded her head as she crossed her legs and then remembered her attire. No bra and skimpy shorts. Not good.

She crossed her arms, the pain to her side instant as she cringed and gasped. He scrunched his eyebrows together and reached for her tank top.

"You're hurt, I can see the blood seeping through your tank top. Let me check it out."

She shook her head.

"You need to let the paramedic look you over," a deep voice stated firmly. She looked up at a very big firefighter with black soot on his cheek. He was attractive, too. In fact, a quick glance around her and she could say with certainty that these were some of the most attractive firefighters she had ever laid eyes on. They reminded her of the men she saw at Sullivan's. Maybe all firefighters and paramedics hung out there.

"I think she's in shock," one said.

"No, she's just shaken up a bit," another added.

"I'm fine." She looked down at her shirt as the paramedic began to pull it up. She prayed that he didn't ask her about the red marks on her forearms from Rico.

"Son of a bitch. You need to go to the hospital," he told her.

She read his nametag. Landers. That was his last name. "No. I don't need a hospital. I'm fine."

He placed his hand on her thigh, and despite the rubber gloves he wore, she still felt a surge of attraction filter into her skin. He held her gaze firmly as if he felt it, too, and then he pulled away quickly. Maybe she imagined it? Maybe it was her weak, insecure mind trying to find safety and security in another male figure? That was stupid, and she couldn't go backward in life and repeat her mistakes. No. She was on her own and no other person, especially a man, was the key to being free and making it in life.

"You are not fine. You may need stitches."

"Stitches? Oh God, how much will that cost?" she asked.

His eyes darkened. "You don't need to worry about that. Let me check it out and see how bad it is."

She nodded an okay and prayed she didn't need stitches. She had nothing. She was homeless and the opportunity to bake and sell her homemade pies was lost.

She covered her face with her hands and leaned back, crossed her legs, and tilted to the side so he could provide first aid. It seemed to her that life sucked and then you die. Maybe it was time to just give in and die already?

* * * *

Johnny Landers was in awe of the gorgeous woman before him. He had never seen her before, and she appeared young, yet mature. She had the most amazing mocha-colored eyes with a hint of glowing color around the edges that made them stand out. Throw in her olive complexion and sexy figure, and yeah, she was a goddess. He swallowed hard as he glanced around, noticing the other firefighters from Engine 20 gathering around. Their chief got them to move away and then raised his eyebrows at Johnny as he glanced at the woman.

"What's your name, honey?" the chief asked her. She opened her eyes and even Chief Sanchez seemed affected.

"Nina," she whispered and then coughed.

"Grab Nina a bottle of water, Caldwell," he ordered to one of his men.

Johnny didn't know why, but he felt sort of strange. It was like he found the woman attractive, he wanted to ask who she was, how long she lived here, if she was single or not, but there was an edge of something. Perhaps just his professional side telling him to heed caution, and of course his past experience with Tara. That bitch really screwed him up and he didn't even sleep with her.

The last thing he needed was some sexual harassment charge against him. The woman was a knockout, though, and he needed to grab a hold of himself and concentrate on providing first aid. It was so odd, but he felt the need to protect as he took in the sight of some older red marks on her forearms. When he raised her tank top up to look at her wound, he noticed traces of similar lines heading toward her lower back.

"Nina, it's not too deep. I can clean it out and bandage it up but you may need a tetanus shot. That fire escape is old."

She shook her head. "No. I'll be fine. Thank you," she said softly, holding his gaze. He brushed his thumb lightly against her skin below the cut and he didn't even realize he was doing it until her eyes widened and her cheeks blushed.

Someone cleared their throat, and when Johnny looked to the right, Chief Sanchez and Chief Martelli were there smiling with their arms crossed in front of their chests.

Mercury handed him a bandage and offered to apply the ointment as he winked at Johnny. It made him feel jealous, which was so bizarre. As he tried to process his thoughts, they heard an explosion and everyone ducked for cover. Johnny pressed his body over Nina's, covering her like a makeshift body of armor. He braced his hands over the back of the fire truck and wedged between her legs, pressing firmly against her body.

"Stay down," he whispered. He could smell her shampoo mixed with smoke. His chin hit her skin on her shoulder and he was so aroused by it. This never happened to him before. Johnny helped to save plenty of beautiful women as a paramedic with Engine 19, but none affected him like Nina.

The chaos of orders being yelled out and firefighters running around grabbing more hose surrounded them.

He confirmed that there were no other injuries and that it was the Dumpster that exploded. Thank goodness no one was nearby, not even the firemen.

He pulled back and Nina's face was covered by abundant chocolate locks of hair. He pressed them away from her face and held her gaze.

"Are you okay, miss?" he asked.

"What was that?"

"Are you two okay?" He heard the voice and recognized it immediately. His brother Trent, the arson investigator for the county, approached.

He saw his brother's eyes lock onto Nina's, and Johnny was immediately thrilled to see the interest.

"We're good," Johnny said and eased away from Nina.

"What did you say that was?" she asked again.

"The Dumpster blew up. No one was hurt though," he told her.

"Hey, I saw you today on the boardwalk, right?" Trent asked, and Johnny looked at Trent then back at Nina. His heart picked up its beat. What were the chances of them both meeting the same woman at different times but the same day?

"I think so," she said and then turned away. Her response either was a sure indication she was blowing them off or she was shy.

"This whole thing stinks. I got Buddy and Jake on their way here now. Once the fire is out, and we know it's safe, hopefully we'll find out who's responsible for this," Trent informed Johnny, his gaze lingering back to Nina.

"Someone caused this fire on purpose?" she asked, sounding as outraged as Trent.

"It seems that way. No need for you to worry, unless you happen to see someone sneaking around here earlier today," Trent said, sounding sarcastic.

"There was some kid, a teenager with a box, by the Dumpster," she replied and then paused, looking around her and then sliding off the truck.

"You saw someone?" Trent asked her very seriously.

* * * *

Nina panicked. These men were so attractive, authoritative, and good looking she lost her ability to think. *Shit! Why did I say that I saw someone? Now they'll ask more questions. Now they'll want my name, my information, and they'll enter it into their computers and Rico will find me.*

"Nina, are you okay?" Johnny asked as he gripped her arm. She was standing up and so were they. Both men towered over her and now Trent was looking over her body. She crossed her arms over her chest in hopes of hiding her aroused nipples from his stare.

She turned away from them. "I'm sorry, who do I speak to about this fire? When can I go back to my apartment?" she asked.

"You may not be able to get back to your apartment at all," Johnny told her. She gasped, the reality of this night was crashing down upon her. She felt her stomach churning, and her heart pounded inside of her chest. She'd lost everything. She had nothing left but what was on her back.

"Oh God." She covered her mouth and closed her eyes. She felt herself losing her balance when strong arms held her and assisted her in to sitting back down on the end of the fire truck.

Johnny covered her legs with his hands as he knelt down in front of her.

"It's going to be okay, Nina. We have a lot of assistance programs here in Treasure Town. You're not alone." He held her gaze.

She shook her head, and tears rolled down her cheeks.

"I am alone, and now I have nothing. Not even the pies I baked for Sullivan's. That was going to be my first job to introduce my homemade pies to the boardwalk. I baked eight pies tonight and they needed to be at Sullivan's by 8:00 a.m. Now they won't hire me. I lost the opportunity because some jerk gets off on setting things on fire? Why is this happening to me? Why? Everything I owned was in that apartment. Including the money from the pies I sold today. There's nothing. Are you sure it's completely destroyed in there?" she asked as she looked up toward the smoking building. There wasn't any more fire but just smoldering ash and firefighters pulling down siding and broken windows. To her the building looked intact and the firefighters did get to the scene quickly.

"That's what you were trying to drag out of there? A bunch of pies you needed to get to Sullivan's?" a firefighter asked, joining the conversation.

She nodded. "I can't believe this is happening." She closed her eyes.

"Let's get back to the person you saw today by the Dumpster. You said you think it was a teenager?" Trent pushed.

"She saw someone? You think it may be our arsonist?" Ace asked as Chief Martelli joined them.

"I didn't see anything. I'm sorry. I was mistaken." She knew she sounded guilty or at minimum like she was lying. She was. She even saw the teen's face and could give a description, but that would bring her more trouble. She couldn't let these men know who she was, her last name, or anything about her. It would only put her in further danger.

"You don't need to be scared, Nina. My name is Trent Landers, Johnny's brother. I'm an arson investigator and we've been trying to track this arsonist down for months. He's caused a lot of damage, but this situation, this fire is the worst. He's stepped it up and someone, you, could have been killed," he told her. She stared at his dark eyes and even darker hair. He was tan and muscular and seemed older in a very attractive way.

"I'm sorry. I can't help you," she whispered. Trent released an annoyed sigh. She kept her head down and shivered until someone placed a blanket over her shoulders. She was shocked as feelings of guilt filled her body. Why should she feel guilty for not helping these men? She didn't know them and she didn't owe them anything. Even though the firefighters rescued her, sort of, she just couldn't help them. It would place her life in danger. Six months she'd been on the run. Six months and no sign of Rico or his crew of thugs. Maybe she'd actually gotten away. No, she couldn't help the arson investigator. This wasn't her problem, her responsibility. Surviving, living was her responsibility. Nothing more.

"Sit back and rest. We'll need to see the damage to the building before we can let you back into your apartment to see if we can salvage anything," Trent told her, and he sounded disappointed. Great, now she could feel guilty and even worse about that, too.

Nina saw two more men walk onto the scene and both wore badges. One was the sheriff. She was immediately on guard. She needed to be smart about this. She had to be.

She watched from the corner of her eye as the sheriff and the other man, who was just as tall and filled with muscles, stood beside him. He glanced at her and she thought he looked familiar. She turned away.

* * * *

"Is the young woman okay?" Jake McCurran asked Johnny, and Johnny nodded.

"She was renting the apartment upstairs. She escaped through the fire escape and made it out," he added.

"No injuries?" Detective Buddy Landers asked, looking back toward her.

"A bad cut on her side but she refused going to the hospital."

Jake thought Johnny seemed upset. "You think she should be going?"

"It's pretty bad, but she signed the papers and I can't force her."

"Who is she?" Buddy asked.

"Don't know. Like I said, she was renting the apartment upstairs. It seems like she lost everything she had. She's pretty upset."

"Damn, well, we'll connect her with Red Cross, and they can assist her, too," Jake said.

"I don't know. She seems suspicious to me. I don't get it," Trent told them with a firm expression on his face as he stared at Nina.

"Suspicious? How so?" Jake asked and Trent explained about her saying she saw someone and then retracting her statement.

"Maybe she's just afraid the person might come after her. Perhaps Buddy and I could talk to her and let her see she would be safe. It would just be an anonymous tip," Jake suggested.

"We can try," Buddy said.

"She's not budging. There's something up with her. Mark my words," Trent added, sounding untrusting.

"We'll try," Jake told Trent and then nodded toward Buddy.

* * * *

As they approached the young woman, Buddy realized why
Johnny and Trent were acting so odd and kept looking over at the
woman. She was extremely attractive. When she turned to look up
toward him, he locked gazes with the most amazing eyes he had ever
seen. They looked like the eyes of a porcelain doll or some exotic
native woman, yet her complexion seemed more Italian than Hispanic
or even Indian.

"Miss, I'm Sheriff McCurran and this is Detective Landers. We
wanted to personally come over here and make sure that you're doing
okay. Is there anything that we can get you?" Jake asked.

Buddy was grateful because right now all he could absorb was the
woman's beauty from eyes and hair to lips and chest. The blanket she
wore over her shoulder was hanging off on one side, revealing more
tan skin.

"I'm fine. Thank you," she whispered and then nibbled her bottom
lip.

Jake pulled out his notepad and a pen.

"I just need a little information from you as we write up a report
of this incident along with Engine 19. Can you tell me your full
name?"

"It's Nina."

Jake raised one eyebrow up at her. "Full name?"

"Do you really need that? I mean what are you going to do with
the information?"

"Are you in some kind of trouble?" Buddy asked her. She gulped
and widened her eyes. She shook her head, but something in Buddy's
gut twisted. Call it instincts from being a detective all these years and
just plain experience. What kind of trouble could this pretty little
young woman be in? He observed her closely.

"Then giving us your name is necessary. We have to cover all aspects of this investigation. Now last name, too," Buddy said.

"Valez," she whispered.

"How long have you lived in the apartment here?"

"Three months."

"Where did you live before?"

She hesitated and looked at Buddy. Again his stomach clenched.

"Where?" Jake pushed in that authoritative way that definitely made most people respond immediately.

Nina looked him over. "What relevance does this have to your arson investigation?" She stood up from the fire truck, letting the blanket fall off her shoulders. Buddy absorbed her figure and the fact that she wore no bra under her tank top. She was well endowed. He was shocked by his body's reaction and the sensation of attraction that hit his chest immediately. He didn't even know who this woman was, and her attitude told him she was hiding something. Trent was right. He focused on Jake's tone.

"Nina, you need to cooperate." Just then someone called out Jake's name. It was Trent and he was waving him over.

"I'll continue with the questions, Jake," Buddy offered and took the pen and pad in hand and looked at Nina. Jake gave her a firm expression before walking away.

"We need to know who you are. It's part of the process."

She looked at him and nibbled her bottom lip. "I'm not involved in the arson investigation aspect of this case. I don't know you, this sheriff, or anyone else around here. I don't see why I have to give all my personal information to strangers."

"We're the law. A serious crime has been committed. You probably lost all your belongings and valuables in that fire and justice will be served. We will find the one responsible for this."

"I'm sorry, but I'm not going to give you my life story. You're right. I probably did lose everything I have in that fire. I even lost the only hope for income, too. Which means I will more than likely have to leave town to find work. I don't have a place to live, these are the only clothes I have…" The tears started rolling down her cheeks and she quickly wiped them and turned away.

"Nina, I'm sorry, but this is protocol. We're going to get you the help you need."

Johnny walked over, joining them.

"I got in touch with Red Cross and the only bed available is a few towns over. But it's a nice place, good people."

"Great. I guess my dreams are destroyed as usual." She crossed her arms in front of her chest and stared at the building that looked bleak on the surface.

Johnny reached out and touched her arm. She jerked away and looked petrified by his touch.

"Hey, we're not going to hurt you. We're the good guys. We're here to help," he told her. She made a snorting sound with her nose and throat.

"Heard that before. Don't worry, I'll manage on my own." She started to walk away.

"Wait. We're not finished here." Buddy stopped her with his firm tone.

"Like it hasn't been enough that I was caught in a fire, I've lost everything, and now you want to harass me, ask me a bunch of questions about things I don't know? I'm sorry, Detective, I don't have anything more to say."

Buddy wondered where her sudden attitude and resistance came from. All he could seem to think was that she was hiding something. Trent mentioned her seeing a possible suspect then retracting her comment. Nina could be the key to finding this arsonist.

"We said that we would help you, and we're going to. That's how things are done in Treasure Town," Johnny told her firmly with his hands on his hips. Even his brother was losing his patience.

"You want to help me? Find me a place where I can bake those eight pies, and provide me with the ingredients I need to do it so I can deliver those pies to Sullivan's tomorrow by eight. That would make me impressed with your Treasure Town."

* * * *

It had been a couple of hours and now Nina walked around the apartment trying to see if she could at least salvage her pie pans and her money. It was early morning and she definitely wasn't going to be able to meet the deadline for making those pies. The tears stung her eyes and she had her hand over her throat as she looked at the mess in the kitchen. Everything was black and covered with soot. The fire had spread through the living room and to the bedroom door. It was eerie how much this apartment, this mess, represented her life. It was black, stuffy with smoke, charred, and terrible tasting as it hit her lungs with every breath she took. It was kind of what she felt like inside right now. Hollow, dark, like life was suffocating her and slowly killing her.

"Anything?" Johnny asked her as he, Jake, Chief Martelli, Buddy, and Trent looked around.

"The pie pans are destroyed," she said, her voice cracking.

"Listen, we know the Sullivans well. The firemen who helped put out the fire tonight are two of their sons. They'll call them and explain," Jake told her.

"There are no excuses for failure," she whispered, the words echoing in her head. That was something Rico would say to her when she complained about messing up a pie she made.

"Don't be so hard on yourself. You didn't do this. Some asshole did," Johnny told her, and she glanced at him. She absorbed the sight of those gorgeous blue eyes she could get lost in if she were normal. But she wasn't normal. She was weak minded, on the run from danger, and a loser with no professional career and no family.

She walked toward the bedroom and saw that most everything was covered in black but the bed was not destroyed all the way through. She had a surge of hope that her money was safe and sound between the mattress as she fell to the floor and lifted up the mattress. She cried, seeing her money intact.

"You keep your money between the mattresses?" Jake asked her.

She looked at him as she pulled the money out and held it to her chest.

"Thank God I did. If I put it in a shoebox in the closet or a jar in the kitchen, it would be nothing but ash right now.

She moved toward the upper part of the bed and the dresser with a renewed inkling of hope that she could stay off the streets for a day or two. She reached under the bed and pulled out her duffle bag. She always had it packed and ready just in case. If she hadn't had the pie order she would have grabbed this and run.

She turned toward them.

"I guess this is where we part ways," she said. All of the men looked at her strangely.

"Part ways? Where do you think you're going?" Buddy asked her.

"I have some money, I can stay off the streets for at least a couple of nights, I have some clothes. I'll figure it out." She started to walk off.

"A hundred-dollar bill is not going to get you far," Johnny said and looked at Buddy, the chief, and Trent. Jake kept his hands on his hips.

"What do you suggest?" she asked.

"That you stay with us," he replied, and she gasped. He quickly began to speak as Jake smirked and walked away. So did the chief. It left Trent, Buddy, and Johnny there.

"Listen, we have a house and a small apartment above the garage. The tenant just left a week ago. It has a kitchen and great oven and stove," Johnny added.

"How much is the rent?"

"We can negotiate when the time comes. You need the help, and we have an empty apartment. What do you say?" Johnny asked. She wasn't sure that this was a wise idea. She didn't want to owe them anything and feel obligated to do whatever they asked of her. They were very attractive men and they seemed sincere, but she had been fooled before. She just didn't know enough about men.

"I don't want to owe you anything. I don't know if and when I could pay you back. You don't know me, and well, I won't let you use this against me to get whatever it is you want."

"What?" all three of them asked. Then Buddy stepped forward.

"You think we would push ourselves on you? That we would expect you to pay us back in some sexual way?" he asked her. The man did not seem to sugarcoat anything, and now that he threw the words out there between them, she felt awful.

She lowered her eyes and nibbled her bottom lip. She just wasn't certain what to do. Was this accepting help from more men a bad decision or a cloud lined with a bit of silver in the shadow of all this darkness surrounding her? It was hard to decline as she stood in the center of a tiny, char-coated room with no place to sleep, no friends to count on, and a fear of what could happen if she let her guard down and slept on some bench in the park. She was tired of that. She never wanted to do that again.

"Sweetie, we're good, honest men. We're first responders in this area. Any of the men and women downstairs right now can vouch for us," Trent added, looking her over, but keeping his distance with an expression that told her he didn't quite trust her or this option his brother offered.

She felt her cheeks warm. The three men were gorgeous and very commanding. It didn't scare her as much as it should have. Instead she felt this tingling sensation, an awareness she just wasn't familiar with.

She crossed her arms in front of her chest.

"I don't trust easy. My past is my business. I won't cause any problems while I stay in the apartment. If I can salvage the job with

Sullivan's and my pie business takes off, then I will pay whatever you guys usually get as rent."

"That's fair enough," Johnny said and reached out his hand for her to take. She stared at it a moment. The skin-to-skin contact wasn't a good idea. She feared being close to any man, never mind touching one.

She looked at Buddy and Trent, who seemed to be analyzing her. Why she had to be in this situation with two investigative minds and one compassionate paramedic she didn't know. She slowly reached out to shake Johnny's hand, and sure enough when their fingers and palms locked, she felt a sexual tingle filter through her body. Johnny smiled.

"You won't regret this."

She barely smiled.

God help me, I hope I don't.

Chapter 4

"Are you serious? How terrible," Florence said to her son Ace.

"Yeah. The poor thing was beside herself. Buddy and Trent think she's completely alone with no family. She had a hundred dollars under her mattress that hadn't burned in the fire, and a bag with clothes stuffed under the bed. Nothing else."

"She spent the last bit of money on the ingredients and pie pans to make the pies for this morning. Oh God, she must be so upset. She doesn't deserve this," Cindy said as a tear rolled down her cheek.

Serefina took Cindy's hand. "Where is she now?" Serefina asked.

"Johnny offered her the apartment above their garage. She didn't seem too keen or trusting, but we all assured her that people were kind in Treasure Town," Ace said.

"They offered her their apartment? Interesting," Serefina said and smiled.

"You think they like her?" Florence asked.

"Oh brother, here we go. I don't know a thing," Ace said as he leaned back in his chair but kept a possessive hand on Serefina's thigh.

Serefina gave him a light tap to his chest. "She doesn't have a job, and no other money, Cindy?" Serefina asked.

"She works a few hours a week at Angel's Wings but the owner can't offer more hours. It's not busy enough."

"I should go by the apartment and let her know that it's okay she couldn't get the pies done. Perhaps she can try again when things get better," Florence said.

"I have a better idea. If this was what she was counting on to make money and support herself, then none of this is her fault." Michaela spoke up.

"Well, she's not very trusting. She had a hard time even accepting the apartment, and Buddy said she thought they wanted something from her in return." He raised one eyebrow up. Serefina scrunched her eyebrows together.

"That doesn't sound good. Maybe Jake was right about her having a troubled past. You said she wouldn't give all her information either?" Michaela asked.

"She's just scared. She reminds me of myself when I first came to town," Cindy offered. "I had a bad relationship, lots of trouble. I thought my life was a mess. But then everyone was so nice here, and I felt so good about things that I started a new life here. Nina is the same. I get the feeling that she's scared, but she's also strong and determined. She's very shy, too. That's why waitressing or doing anything that involves a lot of socializing wouldn't work right now for her."

"I have an idea," Serefina said.

"Oh no," Ace said.

Florence and Cindy smiled.

"What is it?"

Serefina leaned forward and began to explain, and with each detail Cindy and Florence jumped on board to help. Florence was so thrilled that her sons fell in love with Serefina. She was an amazing woman.

* * * *

Nina had a tough time sleeping despite the fact that she felt as if she were in a resort. Johnny, Buddy, and Trent never mentioned that their house was on the beach and that the apartment above the garage had a gorgeous view of the ocean. She kept the windows opened last night and enjoyed the sounds of the small waves hitting the shoreline. This was heaven, but she was scared.

Just like everything else that occurred in her life, the moment she felt confident, a little happy or positive, her world came crashing down.

She had taken a shower and put on new clothes and thought about what she should do first today. She needed to contact Fannie somehow to say she might not make it in to work tomorrow because she was miles from the boutique instead of within walking distance. That was a negative. She would have to see if she could pick up a bike, maybe find one at a garage sale or something.

Just then she heard the knocking on her door.

As she walked through the living room, still in awe of the décor and the beauty of the apartment, never mind the queen-sized bed in the bedroom, she opened the door.

"Good morning."

She was shocked to see Cindy, Florence, and another woman there all holding boxes and grocery bags.

"We heard about what happened. I'm so glad that you're okay," Cindy stated, setting down the bag and pulling Nina into a hug.

Nina didn't know what to do. She didn't quite hug Cindy back but she didn't pull away either.

"We got you a bunch of things to help you get back on your feet and get the business started," Florence said as she began to pull out new pie pans, baking supplies, eggs, milk, fresh fruit.

"Oh God, I can't believe this. I don't know what to say," Nina said, standing there in complete shock. The tears rolled down her cheeks.

"Just say thank you. Oh, I'm Serefina, welcome to Treasure Town." The beautiful woman stuck her hand out for Nina to shake, and Nina reached out and said thank-you.

Florence came over next, held Nina by her arms, and smiled.

"You're no longer alone in this town. You have three new friends, and if those pies come out as tasty as the other day, then you'll have yourself a steady job at Sullivan's as our own local pie maker. We'll order only from you, and cash on delivery. How does that sound?"

Nina was overwhelmed, and without even thinking she hugged Florence who chuckled and hugged her back.

Perhaps things were looking up after all.

* * * *

"She lied about her last name," Jake told Buddy over the phone.

Buddy ran his fingers through his hair as he looked out the back window toward the garage and apartment. He could smell the most delicious scents coming from that direction and he knew Nina was baking pies. He kept making excuses to go outside and sniff the air. She had been at it all day since Cindy, Serefina, and their aunt Florence stopped by with supplies.

"I had a feeling. She's definitely hiding something," Buddy said, feeling his gut clench.

"I can't find out anything about her. It's like she just showed up here a few months ago out of nowhere. I even stopped by Angel's Wings to talk with Fannie Higgins. She said that Nina is a sweet young woman, very quiet, great, hard worker, and she wished she could give her more hours, but the truth was she hired her even though she didn't need help. She felt badly for Nina. When she arrived looking for work, she appeared exhausted and only had change in her pocket for a water bottle from the machine."

"I don't like the sound of that. You think she was homeless or something?" Buddy asked. Saying the words out loud, thinking that was a possibility, upset him.

"Could very well be. She did say she would find a place to stay for a day or so back at the apartment. She had no money other than the hundred dollars. If she's on the run from trouble, we would need her real last name to try to find out more about her."

"Or we could ask her and say we will keep it private. She's scared and untrusting. That's for sure."

"Well, you and your brothers sure did take a liking to her."

"Just as my aunt and Serefina did," Buddy replied, explaining about them dropping supplies off and offering help.

"My God, we've got some great people in this town."

"We sure do. But I don't want their kindness taken advantage of either. If Nina turns out to be some scam artist or criminal, we need to find out before anyone gets hurt," Buddy said, and felt that sensation in his gut chime off that he was totally wrong. Nina wasn't a criminal.

"I'll give you and your brothers a few days to see what you can find out. Then I'll come back over and have to insist she tell us the truth about her last name."

"She really doesn't want any of us to know anything more about her. Trent thinks she saw the arsonist and can describe him but simply is scared about being involved."

"It could be because of what she's running from if that's even the case. She seems really sweet, and she's very attractive. Those eyes of hers are amazing," Jake added.

"I know. But it's odd, it's like I can see how beautiful they are but yet they're filled with sadness. I don't know. Maybe I'm losing my fucking mind?"

"Or you just found the woman of you and your brothers' dreams? It happens just like that. Believe me, it's instant," Jake said and chuckled.

"Like you guys and Michaela?"

"Could very well be, and if you recall, Michaela was pretty secretive when she first arrived. Look where that led."

"Great. Thanks, I'll talk to you soon," Buddy said and disconnected the call.

He put down his cell phone and looked back out the window. He needed to figure out who exactly Nina was. Why did she lie about her last name? What was she so scared of? He was a detective, and he could definitely do this.

* * * *

Nina was exhausted but she'd done it. She'd made a dozen pies for Sullivan's as ordered. As she looked at all of them lined up on the island in the kitchen, she smiled. If this took off, she would have to order some custom boxes with a name on it. That brought tightness to her chest. She always imagined her name on the box and on a storefront. But could she do that or would putting her name out there bring Rico to her door? What would he do if he found her? Would he kill her on the spot? Would he beat her, rape her first since he failed the first time? Would he make her come back to him and to a life of abuse? She felt the tears fill her eyes, and then there was a knock at her door.

She thought it might be Cindy. Nina needed a way to get the pies to Sullivan's. She was in a jam again and would have to rely on help from strangers or her new friends.

She opened the door and was shocked to see Buddy standing there. He looked good. Too damn good for her comfort zone.

"Good morning. Did you sleep all right?" He stepped inside. She closed the screen door, but left the wooden door opened so that she wasn't completely closed inside with Buddy. As much as she wanted to think she was safe, she knew her judgment wasn't good about men.

"Everything was fine. Thank you," she said.

"Wow, you made all these from scratch?" he asked, walking around the kitchen inhaling the smells and smiling. He was truly a handsome man. He had to be in his thirties, a good eight or so years older than her. He was sporting his dress pants, the gun on his hip, his badge, and a dress shirt. He must be heading to work.

She pulled her bottom lip between her teeth and watched him look around and then lean against the counter. He looked her over and she self-consciously tucked a strand of loose hair behind her ear, lowered her eyes, and realized she still wore an apron. She reached back to untie it and pulled it off then held it for support in front of her. Buddy made her nervous for lots of reasons. His authority, profession, and large muscles were effective, much like his height. He had to be at least six two.

"How are you planning on getting these to Sullivan's?" he asked.

"I haven't figured that out yet. I know I need to find a bike or something. Maybe at a garage sale."

He smiled. "You can't stack these on a bike."

"I know that. I meant to get to work at Angel's Wings. I was a couple of blocks away before, but now I'm miles away."

"How did you get there before?"

"Walked."

"You walked everywhere?"

"Yes."

"You don't own a car."

She chuckled softly. "No." She raised her eyebrows and started to wipe down the counter the rest of the way. She realized that he probably thought she was a loser because she couldn't even afford a car, never mind a cell phone.

"I can give you a ride on the way into work. Could you get a ride back here later?"

"You don't have to—"

He raised one palm up for her to go no further. "You just said that you don't have a car. No means of transportation to deliver these pies. I'm offering my assistance. I have a truck and we can load these up, secure them so they stay safe in transport, and then I can drop you off."

"That would be great. Are you sure it's not an inconvenience?" she asked as she prepared to place the pies into a large, wide box.

"I'm sure. Maybe if you're still in town, you can call Johnny or Trent's cell phone and they can drop you back here. I can give you their numbers." He pulled out his cell.

"Oh, I don't have one. That's okay though. I'll find a way back. Don't worry. You guys have done so much, really," she said, feeling badly now for not having the luxury of a cell phone either. "Let me just get washed up really quick before we go."

He nodded his head and she hurried to her room to change and wash up.

* * * *

No cell phone, no car, maybe no driver's license to prove her name as some form of ID. That could be a way to find out who she was. Asking for her ID right now might not be so wise. He looked around the apartment. She had just gotten there last night but already it felt different in here. The last tenant was a teacher at the local high school. He'd gotten engaged a few months ago and moved into his fiancée's apartment so they could save for a house. He was a nice guy but it never felt like this in here. The smell of homemade baking and a woman's scent and feel surrounded him.

"Okay, I'm ready." She pulled on a small backpack then reached into the refrigerator for a bottle of water. He noticed there wasn't much in there aside from a few water bottles and some leftover fruit from the pies.

She went to reach for the large box and he stopped her.

"I'll get it. You get the door. You have the key, right?"

"Yes."

"Okay, let's go.

As they headed toward the truck and he secured the pies, he saw Nina looking at the garage and the set of old bikes. Their mother's bike, the one with the large front basket, was leaning there.

"Are these yours?" she asked.

"Yes, Johnny was going to fix them up and sell them but hasn't gotten around to it yet."

"Would he sell me the one with the big basket? That would be great for me to deliver a few pies or even go food shopping and get to work."

He felt funny about her having to do that. Ride a bike four miles or more to work, to the shop, and to deliver pies.

"I'm sure we can help you out with deliveries as they come."

"Buddy, I appreciate all your help, but like I said at my old apartment, I don't want to owe you guys. I don't know what you expect in return from me. It makes me feel uncomfortable." She lowered her eyes and couldn't look at him. He didn't like the feeling he got, but he needed to gain her trust and play this cool.

"Honey, a thank-you would be sufficient. Ask Johnny about the bike when he gets home from work later. I'm sure he'll work it out with you." She nodded and got into his truck. So much for getting more concrete info on her. All he seemed to do was gain more questions about the woman and wonder why she was so distrusting and resistant to help.

* * * *

Nina was insisting that she would carry the box of pies into Sullivan's herself when the front door to the place opened and Florence, Cindy, Lester, and Al came out to help.

"You made it!" Cindy cheered, and Nina was once again overwhelmed with emotion. She looked at Buddy, and he seemed to stare at her as if contemplating whether she was authentic or not. The man wanted answers. His brothers did, too, as did the sheriff. She wasn't sure how long she could fend them off and avoid answering their questions.

"I hope you like them. I can make just about any pie with whatever fruits are in season," she said as she followed everyone inside. Lester carried in the box of pies.

As they entered, she noticed all the people. Lots of first responders like firefighters, paramedics, police officers. It was a real hangout spot she guessed. The whole idea that she was surrounded by men and women who represented the law had her shaking.

"Al will get your money for you," Florence said, and then Al squinted his eyes.

"Is a check good?" he asked Nina.

She nibbled her bottom lip. "Cash would be better. I haven't gotten around to getting a savings account yet."

She glanced at Buddy and once again his expression intimidated her.

"That's okay. We can do cash. You need to build up your business and then you're going to want to get an account to keep your money safe," Florence said.

"Yes, ma'am," Nina replied. Florence took Nina's hand into hers and she wanted to pull away, fearful of the physical contact, but resisted. Florence was a nice woman, motherly and sweet.

"You call me Florence. We're friends now, remember?" She winked. Nina smiled and nodded.

Before long people were ordering the pies as the aromas filtered through the air. Nina watched in awe as slices disappeared and people complimented her.

"You're going to need some business cards," Cindy said.

"I need a lot more money before I can start doing that kind of stuff. I hope this works out. I haven't even finalized the rent I will need to pay the Landers brothers."

Cindy smiled. "Something tells me that isn't something to worry about." Cindy winked and then walked away to finish working her tables. Nina glanced at Buddy, who was shaking Al's and Lester's hands before he said good-bye.

"Remember to call Johnny or Trent. Florence has their numbers." His expression and his tone were firm and authoritative. It bothered her. She wasn't about to fall back into a routine where men told her what to do and expected her to do it. She was on her own, and no matter what, she needed to remember that. He walked out and Nina remained a little longer. Everyone was just so darn friendly.

A good thirty minutes passed and she decided that she would walk the four blocks to Angel's Wing's to see Fannie. Cindy said she was worried about Nina, and the woman had been so kind to give her that job.

She said good-bye to everyone and told Cindy she would see her in a few days when she visited for lunch, and then she headed out.

* * * *

"What do you mean you didn't give her a ride home? Why not?" Buddy asked Trent over the phone. Trent and Johnny had just gotten home and noticed that no lights were on in the apartment. Johnny knocked on the door and no one answered. He called his brother to see if he knew where she was.

"She never called either of us," Johnny said.

"Where could she be? Where would she go and not tell anyone? I don't like this. I don't like the secrets, the lying about her name." Buddy raised his voice in frustration.

"She lied about her name?" Johnny asked and looked at Trent who now seemed angry.

"What's her real name?"

"I don't know. I think Nina is her real first name but her last was a lie."

"She's hiding something. Definitely," Trent said in the background.

"What should we do? Do we go looking for her?" Johnny asked. Just then the sound of thunder rolling in the background drew their attention.

"Shit. If she's out there, she could get caught in the storm," Johnny said with concern. "I'll swing around past Angel's Wings and see if she's there working. We don't even know what hours she works or what days. We're going to have to find out," he said and then disconnected the call.

Johnny put down his cell phone. He ran his fingers through his hair. "I don't know what it is about her, but she's special. I could tell right away. I have never felt so instantly possessive, protective, or hell, interested like this in a woman."

"It's her eyes, Johnny. Her eyes are stunning. But she has secrets. She could be involved with some guy or something. We have to tread carefully here."

"We?" Johnny asked and smirked as he crossed his arms in front of his chest.

"I'm not saying anything more right now. I admit I was attracted to her immediately. Something drew me in, but I don't play games. Too fucking old and experienced for that kind of shit. Plus this case, this job takes a lot out of me."

"We talked about this, Trent. We talked about our careers, about sharing a woman like our cousins and friends do. Like our parents do out in Fairway. Rarely have the three of us been attracted to the same woman, and even when it did happen it felt nothing like this."

"I know what you're saying. I want answers, too, though. If I'm going to get to know a woman, I need to know who she really is, not who she's hiding behind."

Johnny thought about that a moment and it made sense to him, too. "Should we go look for her?"

Trent mumbled and then stood up. "I suppose we should or we'll sit here worrying until she gets back."

"I'm worried plenty right now," Johnny said and then covered up the food they prepared for dinner. As they headed outside, the rain was coming down hard. He glanced to the right and there was Nina running down the driveway.

"Nina?" Johnny called out as Trent remained in the garage and texted Buddy to tell him she was back.

She ran into the garage, joining them. The woman was soaked, her knee was bleeding, and her clothes were completely see-through. As if noticing them both staring at her nipples, she pulled the shirt away from her body only for it to cling back against a really nice set of breasts. She was voluptuous for such a petite thing.

"Oh God, I thought I would make it before the downpour," she said, water dripping from her hair, down her lovely cheeks between her lips that just asked to be kissed.

Johnny continued his perusal until his eyes landed on her bloody knee. "You're hurt," he said, bending down. He reached for her leg and she stepped back.

"I'm fine. I tripped and fell. It's no big deal, Johnny," she said with an attitude.

Johnny was shocked, but then Buddy pulled up in his truck got out, closed the door, and ran to the garage. "Damn, it's coming down heavy," he said and then took in the sight of Nina. His eyes zeroed in on her breasts, rightfully so, and it was difficult to avoid looking.

She crossed her arms in front of her chest. "Well, I should run to my place."

Buddy grabbed her upper arm to stop her. His expression was of concern. "Where were you? How come you didn't call Johnny or Trent for a ride?"

She pulled her arm from his grasp. "I told you I didn't need to inconvenience them. I had things to do."

"Like what?" he pushed.

"None of your business," she said and stared at him.

He squinted his eyes at her. Johnny knew that both Trent and Buddy had short fuses when it came to being ignored when given an order by them. It seemed that Buddy had been worried about her. He watched as Buddy took a deep breath and released it.

"I'm not trying to boss you around, Nina. We were worried. Last I remember was us talking about you getting a ride from Trent or Johnny. It's a six-mile hike to here from Sullivan's."

"I went to Angel's Wings to see Fannie. She was worried. Then I headed back here after I ordered some things from the farmers market and store near it."

She turned to look at Johnny.

"I was going to ask you if you were selling that bike with the big basket in the front and back. I need a form of transportation."

"We can bring you anywhere you need to go even for deliveries as you get more orders," Johnny told her. She shook her head and stepped back from the three of them. Johnny felt his chest tighten with concern. She was scared of them. Why?

"Are you selling the bike or not?" she asked, crossing her arms in front of her chest. He eyed her over from head to toe and felt his cock harden against the crotch of his jeans. *Damn, she's beautiful.*

"I was thinking about it. I need to fix it up first. It needs some work."

"I can do that. How much?"

"Just take it whenever you need it."

She shook her head. "How much?"

"Nina, it's a hand-me-down. It needs some work and has been sitting there. Just take it and use it."

"I'll work on it tomorrow." She turned to look at Trent and Buddy. "Sorry if I worried you, but I'm not your responsibility. If staying here means you want control over me and to know everywhere I am and who I'm with, then I should start looking elsewhere right away." She started to head out. All three of them were surprised by her statement. Buddy stopped her. He placed a hand on her waist and one against her cheek, cupping it.

"Oh God." She gasped but Buddy remained holding her.

"You're not looking somewhere else. We want you here. We want to be certain that you're safe and that you know you have friends here in town. There's no need for you to feel scared. We would never hurt you, Nina."

She nodded her head, but Johnny could see the tears fill her eyes as she stepped away. "Please don't touch me. Don't say things like that to me. I'm just trying to survive, to live a normal life."

Johnny took her hand and she tried to pull away haphazardly. He locked gazes with her.

"What happened to make you so scared of people? Why won't you tell us your real name? Why won't you let us help you, Nina?" he asked.

She held his gaze and then glanced at the others. "I do alone better, Johnny. It takes more time than most for me to feel comfortable around new people. This attention, all this wanting to help is overwhelming and foreign to me. Where I come from, there is nothing like this. Not the help, the compassion, none of it. People don't care to do things just to make someone feel special or because it's the right thing to do. People expect things in return. They demand and if they don't get what they want, then it's dangerous."

"By people, you mean men?" Buddy asked her.

Johnny's eyes widened. Had a man hurt her?

She pulled her hand from Johnny's and stepped back.

"I'm going to head inside. Please respect my privacy. I need it. I'm not used to having it."

She turned to walk away when Johnny stopped her again. "Nina, let me get you some stuff for the cut. I don't think there's a first aid kit in the apartment."

She ran her hands over her hair and pulled the long brown locks to the side and squeezed out the water. She was shivering.

"We'll see you tomorrow," Trent said, watching her as Johnny handed her a small first aid kit from the shelf. They had a few of them on hand for their trucks.

"Thank you."

They watched her run across the driveway and up the stairs to her apartment. She pulled the key from under her shirt. She opened it, glanced at them, and headed inside.

"What do you think?" Buddy asked.

"Someone hurt her. Bad enough to make her question our assistance. She thinks we're going to expect her to return the favors, and I can't help but to think she means sexually," Trent said in a huff. He turned and headed toward the inside door.

"Fuck, he's right, I get this feeling someone physically hurt her and I don't like the directions my mind is traveling in. I've seen enough crazy shit in this career. Men can be such assholes," Buddy said, walking inside.

Johnny stared back at the apartment. If that was the case and someone hurt her so badly she was adamant about men and relationships, he wanted to change her mind. He wanted to help her heal. Hell, he just plain wanted her. She was sweet, courageous, talented, and a good person. If this was her second chance at establishing a new life, a career, and making it on her own, then having his brothers around to protect her and support her could be exactly what she needed.

Now if only they could convince Nina of that. Then came the fear that she could be pulling some scam over them. Thanks to Tara, he wasn't exactly too trusting either. He hoped that Nina was legit and not about to turn on them, press charges on them, and say they forced themselves on her. Damn, the thought made him feel angry, on edge, and sick to his stomach. He looked back at the apartment, and he thought about Nina and that look in her eyes. She was scared. She wasn't scamming. Something more would come of this. It had to be positive because the thought of not getting closer to her and kissing her made him feel like shit.

Chapter 5

Nina had the worst night's sleep in a long time. She tossed and turned and kept waking up in a cold sweat thinking she had killed Rico and that the police were hunting her down. That led to envisioning Trent and Buddy arresting her and showing their disappointment and hatred toward her. She of course cried in her sleep and felt Johnny comforting her only for him to shove her away when his brothers informed her that she'd killed a man.

It was crazy. She wondered why she kept thinking about the guys. She knew why she dreamt about Rico. She knew that he was alive because if he had died, then the police would have tracked her down months ago. No, he was alive and well and looking for her.

He told her several times that he would never let her go, that she belonged to him, and that he would help her to succeed in her business dreams. She'd bought it all. She'd allowed him to control her, take her mind, soul, and of course her body.

She opened her eyes and looked around the room. She recalled Rico telling her over and over again that he in fact owned her forever by taking her virginity and that no man would ever mean as much to her. He spoke about it often, and would whisper in her ear when they were out in public or at his club.

"You see those women over there? They're nothing but used goods. You, you belong to me now, baby. You gave me the most precious gift that you can only give one time, and it was given to me." She remembered him caressing his palm under her dress below the table and cupping her mound. She felt the tears roll down her cheeks right now remembering his control, his possessive behavior. It made

her feel weak, dependent on him and whatever he commanded. So many times that night when she left, took off scared out of her mind, she debated about returning to him. She thought she needed him to survive and to live.

"You can't ever leave me, baby. There's no reason to. No man will ever touch you as deeply or own you as deeply as I do. There's no use in leaving ever. You understand me, Nina?" he'd asked, pressing a finger under the elastic of her thong panties and stroking her cunt. *"Yes."* She'd submitted back then. The fear of his words and how capable he was had intimidated her. But now as she recalled that moment she instantly felt like shit, knowing how trapped she was back then.

"No other man will ever want you. The more I make love to you, the more I fuck you, the deeper my mark remains inside of you."

"Oh God, will I ever get him out of my head, out of my body?" She covered her head with the pillow and cried.

* * * *

A week had passed and Johnny wondered why Nina hadn't tried fixing the bike. He knew that Serefina stopped by twice to pick up pies for Sullivan's, but it seemed that Nina wasn't showing her face. It bothered him. But Serefina left over an hour ago and he was just about finished cleaning up the bike she wanted to buy from him. He didn't want to take money for it. He would love if she used it. Their mom had left it here years ago.

Just then he heard a door close, and when he looked up, he saw Nina slowly making her way down the stairs.

"Hi, Nina!" he called out and waved. She waved back and slowly headed toward him. When he looked at her, she looked kind of pale and like she lost some weight.

"Nina, are you feeling okay?" he asked.

"You've been working on the bike?" she asked, purposely ignoring his question.

"Yeah, I started it when you didn't come down looking to work on it yourself. Been busy making some pies?"

"Yes. It looks great. What else does it need? I can buy whatever parts are necessary."

"Nina, I said I wanted to give it to you. It was just sitting here anyway."

"Buddy said that you were going to fix them up and sell them."

"Originally I thought about it, but life got in the way. I'm serious now. You can have it."

"That's great. I need to go to the store for some things."

"Do you need a ride?"

"No, that's what the bike is for," she said. When she bent over to see if she needed to raise the seat, she sort of lost her balance. It was like she got dizzy.

Johnny grabbed onto her. "Whoa, are you okay?"

She placed her hand against her head. "Sorry. I think I'm just a little light headed. Like I said, I need to hit the store."

"Have you been eating?" he asked, immediately concerned.

"I'm fine."

"I haven't seen you bring any groceries up except for the stuff for the pies."

"I eat. Don't you worry." She pulled her bottom lip between her teeth.

He reached up and cupped her cheek. "You look pale, and seem weak. Are you eating enough? Three meals a day and lots of water to hydrate?"

"I don't eat three meals a day and I have plenty of water upstairs. There's a thing called a faucet," she replied.

"When was the last time you ate?"

"Last night, dinnertime."

"What did you have?" She tried pulling away as she exhaled in annoyance. "What did you eat?"

"A granola bar."

"For dinner?"

She raised her eyebrows as if saying, "Yeah, so what."

"That's not enough, Nina. Not with working and baking. You need to eat. How the hell are you going to ride this bike five miles to the grocery store? That's insane. Then back here with both baskets loaded up? I'll drive you and help you."

"No, Johnny." She pulled away only for her to lose her balance and almost fall backward. Johnny wrapped his arm around her waist and hoisted her up against his chest. She could have hit the truck. Instead her back pressed against it. He was staring down into her eyes and saw the fear, the weakness in her eyes. They weren't bright. They were sad.

"Nina?" he questioned. When she licked her lower lip and held his gaze, he couldn't resist. He leaned forward and kissed her.

* * * *

Nina didn't know what came over her, but being in Johnny's arms and feeling his masculinity and strength as he kissed her made her forget everything. It lifted her spirits and made her forget why she was depressed and sad. Her weakness from not eating must have weakened her resolve to resist her attraction to him. She wasn't pushing him away or even panicking.

He explored her mouth and ran his hands over her ass, her back, then pressed her harder against the truck. He smelled so good. His cologne was enticing, consuming as it filtered through her nostrils and throughout her body. She pressed her hands against his rock-solid chest and was in awe at his perfect physique. He was gorgeous and sexy, and towered over her, surrounded her with his manliness and capabilities.

But then came the crazy thoughts. The bad memories of the nightmares she experienced night after night. Rico's words, his threats telling her that she would never be accepted by another man again. He owned her, marked her, possessed her, and no one else would ever compare. She applied more pressure to Johnny's chest, indicating for him to stop. Slowly he did, trailing kisses along her jaw and then her neck.

"Damn, Nina, that was incredible." He held her gaze and kept his body pressed against hers. She was locked in place and in shock at what just happened. For the moments when he kissed her, all the fear, all the pain, all the bad memories didn't exist. She was happy.

"Why did you kiss me?" she asked him as she kept her hands against his chest. The solidity and warmth of his pectoral muscles burned through his dark T-shirt and straight against her palms. She was aroused, sexually, emotionally, and she needed to end this before she lost control.

He went to speak and she shook her head. "Forget it. Don't say anything. That can't happen again, Johnny. I'm sorry." She tried pushing away, and he cupped her face between his hands and held her gaze.

"Don't. Please don't push me away after we kissed like that. Nina, you felt it, too. The depth of that kiss, the connection we shared."

"No, Johnny, it's not real. Nothing can happen between us. I'm sorry, but I can't allow it."

"Can't allow it?" he asked, easing his hands from her cheeks and caressing his hands up and down her arms. She wished he would stop touching her so she could concentrate and lie to him. But the feel of his large firm hands gently caressing her skin was too much to ignore. She closed her eyes.

"Oh please, Johnny, I can't give you anything. I have nothing left to give anyone. It's all gone," she said, lowering her forehead to his chest. He caressed her hair and head, kept a hand at her waist, and then hugged her, holding her against him.

"I don't believe that you have nothing left to give. You let yourself go in that kiss and I felt the emotion, the desire. I don't know who hurt you or how he did it, but I'll be damned if my brothers and I are going to let you out of our lives." She looked up at him. "Your brothers?" she asked, shocked by his words.

"Damn straight," he said firmly. She felt her cheeks blush. She knew of ménage relationships. There were loads of them around town. Even Serefina was involved with one. Her men were supposedly cousins with Johnny and his brothers. But she'd never thought about such a relationship. She couldn't even handle one guy's possessive, demanding conditions. How could she handle three?

She shook her head. He cupped her cheeks between his hands again. "Don't overthink this. Don't jump to conclusions. Just feel, Nina. Follow your heart, your gut, your body," he said, looking over her breasts that somehow seemed to have grown in size from his arousing kiss. She felt so much in his kiss. He was right.

She was confused, and now that she was coming back down from the high she was on, she felt sort of light headed. He kissed her softly on the lips. "Come inside and I'll make you something to eat before you pass out. We'll talk about this some more later."

* * * *

Johnny took out the cold cuts and started making Nina a sandwich as she sat on the chair by the island in the kitchen. Her legs were crossed, revealing her sexy toned thighs, and he noticed from the past few weeks since meeting her that she only seemed to have four actual changes of clothing. Plus one navy-blue hooded sweatshirt that had seen better days. It bothered him that she couldn't afford to buy things to wear, and that perhaps she was indeed on the run from trouble. Had she been living on the streets until she got to Treasure Town months ago?

"How long have you guys lived here?" she asked him as she looked around the kitchen. It was an industrial kitchen with a commercial oven, lots of cabinets, all custom designed. They had a built-in bar that overlooked the living room and the beach.

"Well, Trent was here first. This was our uncle's place for years. He moved out to Key Largo to open a bar. Then Buddy and I moved in and we redesigned the entire place. It was outdated," he said, bringing over the sandwiches.

"Have you always wanted to be a paramedic?"

"I was involved with firefighting for a little while, but I guess the paramedic aspect called to me more. I did it as a volunteer for years when I went to college. I wasn't sure medical school would be the right way for me. I guess I like being on the streets in the heat of action."

"Medical school? Wow, what an opportunity." She looked at the sandwich. "I won't be able to eat all this, but thank you for making it."

"You'll eat at least half, and save the other half for a snack later before dinner."

"Dinner?"

"Yes, you're coming over for dinner tonight. I'm cooking steaks on the grill, Trent and Buddy will be here, too."

She shook her head. "No, Johnny. I told you back in the garage that this couldn't happen."

"I know what you said, and what you want to force yourself to believe, but I feel differently here," he said, covering his chest where his heart was with his hand.

She swallowed hard. "Why are you making this so difficult? I can't get involved in any type of relationship."

She took a bite of her sandwich. He did add extra roast beef to hers. It was nice and rare, and if she were undernourished, it would do her body good.

"Says who?" he asked, taking a bite of his own sandwich.

She finished chewing and then looked at him. "My perspective on relationships, intimate or platonic, has changed. I don't think you understand what I'm saying, Johnny."

He looked at her, half smiling while he ate his sandwich. She was so incredibly beautiful, she didn't even know it.

"Baby, listen to me for a moment, okay?"

Her eyes darted around them as if his use of the pet name "baby" affected her. If her red cheeks were any indication or even the way she wiggled around on her seat, he was sure it affected her.

"I don't know what has happened in your past to make you feel this way."

"Johnny, please." She placed her sandwich down. He did the same to his.

"All right. You know what, forget that. Just do me a favor, and let this happen. Get to know us. Learn that we're not bad guys, and that maybe, just maybe something special can happen here."

She was silent a few moments and then she looked at him, pulling her lip between her teeth like she did when she was nervous or scared. "I won't make any promises. This isn't a yes to this craziness. I can't give you what you want, Johnny. I'm incapable. You just don't seem to get that."

He took a deep breath and released it. "Just try. Friends first, okay?"

She stared at him and she nodded her head.

"Let's eat lunch and then fix that bike the rest of the way."

"Yes, I have shopping to do and then work at the boutique tomorrow."

"Do you need a ride there and back?"

She smiled and looked at him sideways. "That's what the bike's for, silly."

He half smiled. Truth was he worried about her. He worried, not knowing who may be after her, what could happen as she rode the bike so many miles, and about how little she ate.

He watched her and wondered if he should ask more questions or if he should leave it alone. Then his phone rang, solving the dilemma.

He answered it.

"Kyle called in sick. I need you in thirty, can you make it?"

"Sure, Chief. I'll be there in thirty," he said.

Nina took a sip of her water and he put the phone down.

"Duty calls. I have to be there in t—"

"Thirty, right?" she said and stood up. "Thank you for the sandwich and for the bike."

"I can drop you off on the way then have Trent or Buddy swing by and get you at the store?"

She shook her head. "No thank you. Be safe." She started to walk away and he hurried around the island. He stopped her by taking her hand into his.

He reached up and gently stroked a finger against her cheek. "Be careful on the bike." Before she smiled fully he leaned forward to kiss her good-bye.

* * * *

"We've been over these video surveillance tapes a dozen times. He's not on there," Buddy said while Trent and Jake both looked annoyed.

"We don't have any leads whatsoever. No one has seen anyone suspicious walking around before the fires. Plus, whoever is responsible, they're covering their tracks pretty well. The evidence left behind is nearly fully destroyed. It's taken these last three weeks for the lab to confirm the substance used to cause the explosion in the Dumpster," Trent added.

"What was the chemical used?" Jake asked.

"Here, it's a combination of various cleaning agents. Nothing that is unique or isn't readily available from wholesale industrial cleaning supply companies," Trent told them.

"Can a regular consumer buy this stuff in the supermarket?" Jake asked Trent.

"Probably not. It's more readily available in office buildings, schools, places where there's a custodial staff that takes care of housekeeping. Why, what are you thinking?"

"You need to talk to Nina again. What if what she blurted out was true about seeing a teenager? Maybe she did actually see our arsonist," Jake said.

"And I need to talk to her and ask her again so she can just deny it and not answer my questions again?" Trent asked.

"Because she's renting an apartment on our property," Buddy said and stared at his brother.

"Or simply because the three of you like her, and she more than likely likes you but is young, scared, and you're a lot older than her. As soon as she saw my badge, she got all nervous. She might have an issue with authority," Jake stated.

"Like she's been locked up or something?" Buddy asked.

Jake raised his eyebrows as he stood up straighter.

"No one knows anything about her. She lied about her last name, refused Red Cross and going to the hospital for her injuries. I'd say she was avoiding having her information put into a computer system."

"I thought about that, too. But why? What could happen if her name is in a hospital admittance log?" Trent asked.

"It gives whoever may be looking for her a way to track her down. Even if they Google searched her name or the word hospital, injury, a list of matches could show up. By outing her name in the system, it risks being found," Buddy said to his brother.

"I haven't liked this situation from the start. She's gotten away with pushing us back, only giving little bits of info and then shutting down. What if she's involved?" Trent asked.

"It's our job to investigate all our leads. You've given her more than ample time to get used to you, Trent, Buddy, and even the community. She needs to answer the questions. You need to confront her on this," Jake said. Just then their cell phones and radios went off.

"We got a suspicious fire on Bullson Street. A 911 call came in giving a description of the individual seen running from the scene," Jake stated.

"We need that witness. Let's go," Trent said. He and Buddy headed out of the office with Jake.

* * * *

Nina was shaking. She couldn't believe her luck. Just as she left Angel's Wings and headed down the side streets instead of the main roads because the traffic was so busy, she spotted the person in the red jersey again. This time his hair was hidden, and she couldn't tell if it was the same blond-haired kid. Her gut told her yes, and suddenly as he sprinted across the parking lot, she heard and saw the Dumpster by the side of the building explode. She covered her ears and as things settled down she saw some people lying down in the parking lot, injured. She ran to the pay phone and called 911 immediately. She couldn't leave her name or say who it was or the police might think that she was involved. If she learned one thing living with Rico and hanging out at the club listening to the men talk about evading police, she learned that once you were on the cops' radar, they never let up.

She knew that Buddy and Trent didn't trust her. That was what made the situation with Johnny even more intense today when he kissed her. He mentioned his brothers wanting her, too, and all she could think was that they were along for the ride. Neither man expressed any romantic interest even though she caught them watching her and eyeing her body over several times when they thought she wasn't looking. They affected her just like Johnny had. But they were commanding, controlling, expected order, respect, and submission. All those things led to dominance and abuse and eventually a cheating man. As it was now, she wasn't even good enough for them. Just as Rico had pounded into her.

She pedaled faster, trying her hardest to get back to the apartment. Another two miles and she would be there.

God, I hope no one was hurt in that blast. At least I called the police and gave a description. They'll never find out it was me.

* * * *

"Calm down, Trent. Don't jump to conclusions," Buddy told his brother as they searched for Nina on the way back to their house. They knew she rode the bike.

Buddy wondered why the hell Johnny let her take it if he knew she would be working until nine in the evening. That was dangerous in itself. But now, after heading to the scene of the explosion in a Dumpster by a school building, then hearing the 911 call, and identifying the woman as Nina, they needed answers. Jake was ready to haul her in for questioning. She was the only witness they had.

"Shit, we must have missed her," Trent stated as he came up onto their driveway. "Unless she's already home?" Buddy suggested.

"You think she made it six miles on a bike back here that quickly?"

"If she was scared, adrenaline pumping, worried about making the call and being identified, sure. I think she could have."

"You see what I see?" Trent asked as they parked the truck in front of Nina's garage and apartment. They both saw the one light on.

Trent turned off the ignition and got out of the truck quickly.

"Trent, we don't know how involved she is in this. She could really just be a witness, you know, in the wrong place at the wrong time?"

"Or she could be involved, which is why she won't tell us her name or anything about her life, where she came from, how she doesn't have a license, identification, bank account, cell phone. Need

I go on, Buddy?" Trent asked. Buddy shook his head. Now he was getting angry, too. As they climbed up the steps, Buddy felt on edge.

"Remember what Johnny told us about today. About the progress he made with her."

Trent shot him a look. "None of that will matter if she's a criminal."

Trent knocked on the door pretty hard. There wasn't an answer, but then they both heard something drop.

* * * *

Nina had just got out of the shower. She couldn't believe she saw the person responsible for the explosion in the Dumpster and that it appeared to be the same person who caused her building to go up in flames. She just wrapped a towel around herself when she heard the banging on the door. She gasped and knocked over the bottle of shampoo, making it fall into the tub. She just bought that today.

Holding the towel against her body, she could see two large figures outside her front door. She freaked out, looking for something to defend herself with and couldn't help but think it was Rico or his thugs.

A moment later, as she held one of the pie pans as her weapon, the door opened, and Trent appeared, gun, badge, and all.

"Jesus, Nina, we thought you were in trouble," Buddy said as he put his gun back into the holster. She was shocked that they were there and broke into the apartment.

"What's going on? You scared me. I thought you were intruders," she said as both men looked her over. Buddy ran his hand over his mouth and she remembered she was standing there in only a towel.

"Oh God, I need to get dressed. I just finished showering."

She turned to head into her bedroom when Trent spoke up.

"We have questions for you, so get dressed quickly and then get out here so we can talk."

* * * *

"Did you see her back?" Buddy asked Trent and Trent just nodded slowly.

"What do you think those marks are from?"

"I don't know, but we're not leaving here until we have answers to our questions and we're satisfied."

Nina came out a few minutes later wearing one of the four outfits she always wore. It seemed to Trent that maybe they were all she owned. That bothered him. She was such an attractive woman and deserved to have more.

"Nina, why don't you take a seat so we can talk." Trent motioned with his hand for her to sit on the couch. She did, wringing her hands together along the way. When she sat down, he saw the bandage on her knee from the other night when she walked home in the rain and fell.

He swallowed hard. Buddy took a seat across from her and Trent stood with one hand on his holster.

"There was a fire tonight. An explosion in a Dumpster a couple of blocks from Angel's Wings."

"Really?" she asked. He widened his eyes and she looked back down at her hands. He could tell she was nervous. He really hoped that she wasn't involved. He liked her, was attracted to her despite the age difference. She had it rough, it seemed, and that bothered him a lot.

"Nina, we know that you left work at nine. We know that you made a 911 call to the police identifying the one who set off the bomb and also asking for help for injured people in the parking lot."

She shook her head. "I don't know what you're talking about."

He could hardly hear her. He flexed his muscles, clenched his teeth, and then calmed his annoyance with her lies. "Nina, you're not in any trouble. We just need the truth. Right now the sheriff wants to haul you in for questioning. Others think you could be involved with these arson fires," Trent told her, and she immediately shot her head up in shock.

"Me? I didn't do anything. Is this how you police operate around here? You accuse the ones who identify the criminals and call 911 for help when they see people injured and then you blame them? Fucking incredible." She stood up. Before she could move Trent grabbed her upper arm and locked gazes with her. She was all fired up and he was angry, confused, and even aroused being this close to her and inhaling her perfume and shampoo.

"You were the one who made the call for help?"

"Yes, I made the goddamn call, but no, I am not involved. Are you out of your minds? I was the one who saw him and called it in immediately. I saw people lying on the ground and I feared they were seriously hurt. I didn't have a cell phone so I used the pay phone. Now you want to pin this on me?"

"Why don't you have a cell phone?" he asked. Nina looked shocked. Even Buddy was a bit taken back by his brother's redirection of questioning.

"I don't need one. I can't afford one. It isn't necessary. Does that make me a criminal, too, Trent?" she asked with attitude.

He pulled her closer. "Don't test my patience, Nina. I want answers now. What's your last name? The real one." She shook her head and tried pulling away. "Where did you come from? What are you running from?"

"Stop it. Just stop asking me questions that aren't any of your business." She raised her voice and pulled from his grasp.

"Don't walk away from me, Nina. We're the good guys."

"Ha!" she said as she turned to look up at them. "You're just like every other man. You're just like him. You come in here and make your demands and threaten. You want to lock me up on bullshit, then do it. Put me in jail. I'll probably be safer in there," she said, her voice cracking.

"What does that mean?" Trent asked her.

"Someone hurt you? Was it a man, a boyfriend?" Buddy asked, and Trent grew angrier. Could the marks on her back and her forearms be from the guy who hurt her?

"Why do you want to know? Why do you need to?" she asked as she sat back down on the couch.

"Because we care about you. We want to get to know you. Johnny explained it today."

"I can't be what you want me to be. What he wants. I'm not good enough for one of you, never mind three."

"What? Are you out of your mind?" Buddy asked, moving next to her on the couch.

She looked at him and then closed her eyes. "I'm nothing, no one. I'm just trying to live. It's all I want to do is survive and be free. But everything around me turns into a problem, a conflict, a disaster. It's like I'm destined to fail, no matter what. It's him. He warned me. He told me that I would be nothing without him. I'm not saying any more."

Buddy covered her knee with his hand and leaned closer. "Nina, you're not making any sense. We're both trying to understand what's going on here. Help us. This guy, whoever he is from your past, obviously did a number on you. We can handle that. We can work through that. But right now we need to know if you're involved in these arsons or if you can help us stop this individual who's committing these crimes. Please, you can help and it can save lives."

Slowly she looked up toward him with tears in her eyes. She stared at his face as if she were absorbing every line and wrinkle, or perhaps she was searching for safety in his eyes. Buddy wasn't sure but he was losing his patience and he was also feeling more and more attracted to Nina.

"Answer him, Nina," Trent said. Hard-core, demanding, get-what-he-wants-when-he-wants-it Trent.

She stirred slightly at Trent's tone but remained looking into Buddy's eyes.

"I saw the one you're probably looking for. It's a teenager. The night of the fire at my place he was wearing a red jersey with the word Costa or something on the back in white letters. He also had a baseball cap on. The Yankees. He was five feet seven, and blond hair was coming from his cap. He carried a box and put it near or in the Dumpster. Tonight when I left work, I took the back side streets because the main road was too crowded, and even on my way this afternoon I was nearly hit by a car."

Buddy was concerned about that, too. At least she took precautions.

"Was it the same guy tonight?" Trent asked, but she wouldn't look at him. She held Buddy's gaze. He gave her knee a gentle squeeze. "Nina?"

She shrugged her shoulders. "I'm not a hundred-percent sure. It was kind of dark but his movements, his body in the clothing looked similar. But I couldn't make out the blond hair. Maybe it was tucked under his hat this time. But he did the same thing. He put some box or something in the Dumpster, and then he turned, and it seemed like he looked right at me because I stopped the bike on the sidewalk and watched him. Then he sprinted. I looked around and there were people there, you know, heading to their cars or walking from the school when the explosion sounded. I saw people on the ground and I immediately ran to the pay phone, called the police, and then left." She lowered her eyes and looked down at her hands.

"Nina, you did the right thing. You called for help and you left the description of the criminal involved. But you didn't have to run. The police, Trent, Jake, and I would ensure your safety."

She shook her head and seemed to be shaking. He could feel her leg moving.

"She couldn't, or her information would go into the system and this guy, whoever it is she fears, could find her," Trent stated. Nina looked right up at him. His arms were crossed, and his intense stare even hit a nerve with Buddy.

They were all silent and then Nina stood up and started walking away.

"You got what you wanted. This should be enough. There had to be other witnesses this time. Interview the victims, the ones who fell to the ground. They were closer than I was."

Trent grabbed her hand. She paused and looked up at him.

"The questions aren't over."

* * * *

Nina was just about feeling numb. She really wanted to trust them. She wanted them to know who she was, where she came from, and how hard her life had been. Not because she wanted sympathy but because she felt terrible lying to them and hiding who she was. Maybe if she told them, they would see that she was trash, worthless, and used goods, as Rico called her.

But they were so attractive and strong. A tinge of hope that they could care, truly care about her, filtered through her body. She felt empowered around them and capable. Everywhere else she felt weak and vulnerable. But how could that be? She barely knew them.

Just looking over both men made her heart hammer inside her chest, and her body reacted, too. They were attractive, muscular, and even now, late at night with Trent in need of a shave, he looked rugged and capable. Even in the dress shirt, his neck muscles and traps, she thought they were called, stood out. His muscles had muscles, and his dress shirt didn't hide his physique. Add in the gun and the badge and she was shaking like a leaf.

"I will not hurt you. We won't put you in harm's way. Our questions now are for us to know. For Johnny, Buddy, and I to know the woman we want is real and not lying to us."

She shook her head. "You don't want me," she said, her voice quivering with emotion.

He pulled her closer, ran his hand under her hair to the base of her head, directing her to look up at him. Standing here barefoot, he towered over her and represented all she feared. The capabilities of a man, a trained law enforcement officer, both aroused her and scared the heck out of her. With her oversensitive breasts pressed snug against his iron-hard chest, it wreaked havoc on her brain. She lost all control to fight this attraction and to not let him get closer. Then it was too late. Trent covered her mouth and kissed her.

Unlike Johnny, who took his time and progressed to a deeper kiss with ease, Trent went full throttle. He stroked his tongue deeply, his one hand held her head in support and in a dominant way that somehow didn't cause fear and instead caused arousal. When he used his other hand to move over her ass to squeeze her closer to him, the significance of the difference in size between them made every feminine part fill with excitement. She moaned into his mouth and was lost in his kiss when suddenly she felt a second set of hands on her hips. She knew Buddy joined them, as she felt his firm, hard body pressed against her back. His cock, long, hard, and thick, fit snugly against her ass and wild ideas filled her mind. Being taken sexually by three men would mean anal sex. At least Rico hadn't had time to force that upon her, too.

With thoughts of Rico came fear and inadequacy. Despite what she thought about these men's sexual experience and extent of women they shared, she still felt undeserving of them and their attention.

She pulled from Trent's lips and panted for breath as he held her close, her mouth now against his neck. She felt Buddy's lips kissing her shoulder, then her neck before she could tell them she needed a reprieve, time to think and process this, time to push them away out of her own fears and past indiscretions. Buddy turned her face toward him and kissed her.

Trent released her to his brother and she turned in Buddy's arms as he pulled her tight against him and devoured her moans. She was beyond overwhelmed, she was on a high, off this planet and in a place she wished she could be forever. It was so dramatic, so deep and emotional that she hadn't realized she was crying until Buddy released her lips and hugged her tight. He caressed her back, her head, and her shoulders.

"It's going to be okay. Don't cry," he whispered, his warm breath against the top of her head.

"My God, Nina, what did this guy do to you?" Trent asked, and she squeezed Buddy tight.

"He took everything. My heart, my soul, my body, and ruined it for anyone else. Alone is where I belong. Alone." She muffled her anguished cry against Buddy's shirt and solid chest. To feel him for just a few more second would have to last her a lifetime in her lonely world. It was how she thought it needed to be.

* * * *

Buddy locked gazes with his brother Trent over Nina's head. He continued to hold her, and Buddy could tell that Trent was not going to accept Nina's response to them. Not when she just kissed them the way she did, and they obviously both felt the same chemistry. Johnny did, too, and if he were here right now he wouldn't stand for it. Trent was the hard-ass of the family. He was the demanding one and expected a lot in a woman he bedded, but this was more. Nina was more than just a woman they wanted sexually.

They were attracted to her in all aspects, and the key part that made this so different was that the three of them wanted her. She was what they hoped they could find one day. A woman who would allow three men, three brothers, to love her, cherish her, and care for her in every way. Nina's defiance, stubbornness, and self-sacrificing days were over.

"Your response to our kisses is unacceptable," Trent stated before Buddy could suggest that they sit down and talk things through. Despite being a bit of a disciplinary himself, Buddy was also pretty diplomatic about things. He never jumped the gun and he always looked for the signs, the things one least expected before he jumped to conclusions. It was part of his career as a detective.

Buddy felt Nina cling to him and then abruptly pull away. She backed up until her rear hit the end table and Trent made his move.

"Don't look at me like that. Don't look at me like I could hurt you."

* * * *

Trent wasn't sure what to think. He was fighting with himself about how to react to a number of things. His feelings for Nina, the desire to make her his and his brothers', and the need to take the fear away and to know what happened to her to make her feel so inadequate. She was insecure, fearful, timid and lacking in self-confidence. As an older man with more experience, he couldn't help but to think that Nina was abused. Perhaps even raped. It made him sick with anger. But he also had his brothers to look out for. Johnny was already so into her that if she took off or simply negated their advances, it would hurt him.

She gripped the wood on the end table and stared at him with such fear that her face looked pale. He didn't look at Buddy. This was his job as the oldest male to handle a situation like this. If Nina wasn't ready to accept their help, their affection, then they would have to leave her alone.

"You're being aggressive. You're trying to control me and make demands. I'm confused."

"Look at me. Look at me, Nina," he stated firmly. She did immediately. He held her gaze and absorbed the site of her mocha eyes, the fear and sadness in them. It tugged at his heart but he needed to be firm. He needed her to know she was safe with them.

"My brothers and I will not hurt you. We don't hit women, we don't force ourselves on them. That's not our thing. We're older than you, I understand your fears, and I think, if my gut is right, someone, a man, abused you." Her eyes widened, her lips parted as if she was going to deny it, but then she stopped and he continued to speak.

"Perhaps he even forced himself on you, used you and that innocence you still seem to display, because that's who you are."

Her eyes welled up with tears. He was right on the money. He needed to ignore the pull toward anger to know who the fucker was who did this to her. To such a sweet, vulnerable, young woman like Nina.

"Maybe you've been on your own, took off, left him because of the abuse and you've been running since. Am I close?" he whispered, stepping closer. Easing his way near her so she would feel his masculinity and perhaps find strength in it. The thought seemed pompous, but he was following his instincts, and they had yet to fail him with Nina.

She swallowed hard. "I don't want to talk about him," she whispered.

"I think you need to explain it to us so we can understand."

"Why?"

He took a deep breath and released it as he eyed her over. The woman was built for him, for his brothers. She had everything they desired in a lover.

"Because we care, and we like you. We feel an attraction to you and we want to explore that attraction. You feel it, too, Nina."

She shook her head slowly.

"Nina, I felt you clinging to me when I kissed you. Your eyes were closed, you moaned into my mouth. We can't fight what's right there in front of us. This is real. Take the chance and let us in."

She reached up to cover her mouth and suppress a cry.

"Baby, please let us in. Talk to us and make us understand your fears. We'll help you every step of the way," Buddy added.

She looked at him. "I've seen guys like you with all the women. You're older, more experienced, and you'll expect things. I'm not like those women. They cling to you, vie for your attention, they want you because of your careers, your masculinity and you—"

"Don't want them, we want you," Buddy said.

"What you say may be true. Our careers tend to attract a lot of women, but that doesn't me we act on them. As a matter of fact, the three of us, Johnny included, haven't been intimate with any woman in months. Don't hold it against us. It's a silly thing to fear. We get that you're inexperienced when it comes to men and trusting your emotions, your body with them," Trent said.

"Men?" She shook her head and pulled her lips into a tight line as she lowered her eyes.

Trent squinted his eyes at her. Looked her body over. She couldn't be so inexperienced that she knew so little about sex and relationships. Why did he suddenly feel like he was capable of hurting her due to her fragility? Part of him wanted to step back and give her some time to adjust and the other part felt so possessive. The more she revealed about herself and her fragility, the more protective he became.

"We don't want those other women. We want to get to know you, learn about you in every aspect," Buddy told her. She looked so lost. She stared between Trent and Buddy.

"He had other women around him, too. He told me all the time it was only me he wanted, me he cared for. I was foolish enough to believe him, to feed into his control and allow him to own me. He proved he didn't want only me."

"He cheated on you?" Trent asked, teeth clenched.

"The woman I found him with said that I was too sweet, too regular to provide him with the wild things he liked to do in bed. He took my virginity and said he owned me, all of me, and no other man would ever want me, never mind have me."

"Asshole," Buddy whispered. She looked at him, then toward Trent before she started to lower her eyes and fidget with her hands.

"You don't believe that, do you, honey?" Buddy asked.

Trent reached out and brushed his thumb and pointer finger against Nina's cheek and chin when she didn't reply.

"Dominance and control, manipulation of the mind of one so innocent. He's the one who broke down your self-esteem, made you timid, scared of a man's touch and affection. He can't get to you now. He can't have what's ours."

She blinked her eyes. "I'm not yours. Didn't you hear what I just told you? I gave him my virginity. He said he owned me and that no other man would want me or have me."

The tears rolled down her cheeks. Buddy took her hand and squeezed it.

"We want you. We care about you. They were all lies by him to control you. He probably said it over and over again, maybe even whispered into your ear when you were out in public as a reminder of his dominance and control," Buddy said.

She gasped and tried to hold back a cry.

"Is that what he did, Nina?" Trent asked. She nodded her head.

He cupped her cheek and held her gaze.

"Lies. They were all lies for him to show power over you. He can't control you anymore, Nina. He's not here."

"He's in my dreams, my nightmares. His words pop into my head throughout the day. I don't have control over that fear because I know he's coming. I know he's looking for me."

"How do you know? You escaped his grasp. You got away, and you ended it." Buddy looked at her waiting for an answer.

She was quiet a couple of seconds and then she whispered.

"Because I nearly killed him."

* * * *

Buddy was shocked by her statement. He locked gazes with his brother, who pulled Nina into his arms and hugged her. She looked so fragile and petite in his arms. He reached out, even though her statement instantly shocked him and made him have further questions, he also felt even more compelled to protect her and to ultimately take the pain and fear away.

"Let's sit down and talk," Trent suggested and led her to the couch. He sat first and didn't release her hand. Then she sat down. She rubbed one hand up and down her thigh over her knee as Trent held her other hand. Nina took a deep breath before releasing it.

Buddy sat down on the coffee table in front of Nina. He covered her hands with his, caressed them until she looked up at him. Trent was rubbing his hand up and down her back.

"Okay, let's talk this through so we understand the level of danger you might be in right now."

"Danger level?" she asked.

"Yes," Trent said and caressed some of her hair away from her cheek. She glanced to the left and looked at him.

"We're investigators, it's what we do. Let us evaluate the situation. That's a first step in the right direction of you trusting us."

"I didn't say that I don't trust either of you. I want to. I feel good with you. Safe, ya know?" she said and shyly looked down.

Buddy reached up and gently brushed her chin and lower lip with his thumb as he smiled.

"Safe is good. That makes us happy. Now, tell us where you lived before Treasure Town."

There was suddenly a knock on the door and Nina gasped and jumped back against the couch. Trent held her by his side, and Buddy patted her leg. "It's okay. We're here and you're safe, remember?" He walked toward the door, feeling on edge even though Nina only told them minimal information about this guy possibly coming after her.

He kept his hand on his revolver. When he opened the door, Johnny was standing there. He looked so worried.

"Is she okay? What the fuck happened? I just got off work. Kyle came in for his shift. I heard about the Dumpster explosion and then Jake said Nina was involved." He walked in and went right to Nina.

Buddy closed the door and locked it as Johnny went to the couch, knelt down on the rug, and pulled Nina into his arms.

"Are you okay? Did you get hurt?" he asked, caressing her hair and her cheeks as he pulled back to look at her.

"I'm fine."

"We discussed a lot with Nina, Johnny. Take a seat. Nina's about to tell us about her life before moving here and about an ex-boyfriend who may or may not be looking for her," Trent said.

"What?" Johnny asked, looking from Nina to his brothers then back toward Nina.

"Your brothers thought I was involved with the explosion tonight because I called 911 and reported the explosion, the people injured, and gave a description of the teenager I saw running from the scene before it detonated."

"Shit. You wouldn't leave your name? You didn't want to be placed into the computer system?" he asked, but it was more like a statement. They all knew the answer.

Nina lowered her eyes and then looked back at Buddy. He gave her a nod.

"Explain about this ex-boyfriend and about how you escaped."

Johnny heard the word "escaped" and ran his fingers through his hair, giving Buddy a firm expression. Buddy just stared at his brother. He prayed that Nina wasn't a criminal or on the run from police. It would kill Johnny, never mind upset Buddy and Trent.

"I lived in California. A shitty part. I grew up with nothing."

"No family?" Trent asked.

She looked at him. "None worth mentioning, except for Cleo. He helped raise me. If not for him I would have wound up in foster care or dead on the streets. I learned pretty quickly that in order to get out of the neighborhood and not wind up like my mother, I needed school and work."

"He was a stepfather?" Johnny asked her.

She shook her head. "Nope, he was a man my mom was seeing until she broke things off. She cheated on him, liked drinking, partying, and eventually prostitution. Cleo couldn't just leave me there in the apartment. I was thirteen. He saw the way men looked at me and he pretty much became my protector."

"He stayed there with you, in the apartment?" Buddy asked, not understanding how this stranger could just take over and her mom not intervene or act concerned. She was her mother.

"My mom was never around. She hardly ever came home and sometimes if she did come home, she wasn't alone. It became dangerous for me." She twisted her fingers together. She was obviously nervous.

"Did any of those men force themselves on you, Nina?" Trent asked. He was definitely in detective mode as Buddy should be. But all he kept thinking about was this poor little girl who no one loved or cared about. How sad.

"Cleo wouldn't let that happen," she said, her voice cracking with emotion. She obviously trusted Cleo enough to accept his care for her.

"This guy Cleo took you to his home?" Trent asked.

She nodded. "Cleo was a good man. He worked odd jobs but had some money set aside. He had a sister with kids an hour or so away from his place that we visited a couple of times. He was trying to give me a normal life."

"What happened to your mom?" Johnny asked her.

Nina leaned back against the couch, crossed her legs, and took a deep breath before releasing it.

"She's dead. I stayed living with Cleo and he helped find me some jobs working in local stores, helping to clean houses in better neighborhoods. I have my diploma because he pushed me to finish school and follow my dreams of becoming a baker. Cleo had some of his own problems, though."

"Problems?" Johnny asked.

She looked at him. "Gambling. He got in over his head a few times. But it eventually killed him two years ago."

"What do you mean?" Johnny asked.

"He was killed because he owed a debt," Trent stated. He didn't ask and Nina didn't say a word. It was another sign of her natural defense mechanism to not give up information unless forced to, and not allow herself to feel when she was trying so hard to be strong.

Buddy saw her lip quivering. He had an overwhelming urge to pull her into his arms and tell her that everything was going to be okay. But they still needed the whole story.

"That must have been tough. What did you do next?" Trent asked.

"Well, before he died we used to go down to the park sometimes. I would meet him there after work. He's the one who got me a job at a local bakery. He knew I would love to make pies. I dreamed of being a baker, having my own business someday, but life just got in the way, ya know? My friends were all older, more experienced in life. They took me under their wings, introduced me to people, and sometimes if I wasn't too exhausted after work we'd go out to the clubs."

"Is that where you met the guy?" Buddy asked her.

"I thought it was fate."

"Fate?" Johnny asked.

She looked away, past Trent's shoulder as if remembering the moment she met the guy, and it bothered Buddy. It made him feel jealous and possessive. He needed to tread carefully here. He was liking her too much already, and too soon.

"He appeared out of nowhere. He approached me and started talking. He was very attractive, a few years older, and he was the owner of the club."

"Under thirty and he owned the club?" Trent asked, sounding suspicious. He was probably thinking what Buddy was, that this guy was into something illegal, unless he came from money. That would be a reason for any young innocent woman who came from nothing to be attracted to him.

"He was into different things besides the club business. I don't know what exactly, and he never let me onto any of it. He just paid attention to me. Said things to me no one ever said before."

"We get it. He manipulated you into thinking that you were special and that you would be his only woman," Trent said, sounding as jealous and angry as Buddy was.

"I understand that he used me. I get that. I got it really clear six months ago when I showed up at his penthouse and found him with another woman."

"Damn," Johnny stated aloud.

"Penthouse? How wealthy was this guy?" Trent asked.

"Wealthy. Within the year or so we were together, he seemed to really be doing well with the club. In fact, he had promised to fund the place I wanted to open to sell my pies. He encouraged me to practice, paid for me to take some classes, and had a friend of his, a business guy, look into financing a storefront in a great location. It was coming. We even looked at the storefront together a week before that day I found him cheating."

"What happened that day you found him, Nina? You told us that you thought you killed him?" Buddy asked her. Johnny swung his head toward Buddy, but Buddy kept his eyes glued to Nina's.

"I was shocked, hurt, extremely sick to my stomach as I opened the door to see him kissing her. She was fixing her dress, and he had no shirt on. He had lipstick on his chest and neck. She immediately got out her claws, told me that I was too sweet, too innocent to satisfy him in bed so he needed to look elsewhere for what he wanted. The sight of her, this woman I had seen so many times before that he made me think was just an acquaintance, was his side lover. He probably had more. The thought made me feel so sick, to think how he catered to me, expressed his love and commitment, especially because he owned me fully since I gave him my virginity. He used that to manipulate me and control me, like you both said. I was sick, disgusted, so hurt that I threw up all over the woman."

"What?" Buddy asked. He was surprised. Johnny chuckled.

"That must have been a sight."

Nina chuckled. "I can laugh at that now, but it was another show of weakness, fragility, like you said, Trent."

Trent looked at her with an expression of guilt for describing her in that way. But he was right, and because of that weakness Nina suffered greatly.

"I'm sure he didn't mean it so negatively," Johnny said and glanced at Trent.

Nina locked gazes with Johnny. "Trent was right. His description accurate. I can see that now, and because of the experience, it's made me distrust people more and more."

"You can trust us though. We're not like that," Johnny told her. Buddy knew that his brother was in deep. He never saw him act like this, so into and consumed by a woman so quickly, especially after what Tara did to him. His brother would lose it if this was some sort of trap or game Nina was playing. But his gut was usually pretty accurate. So much so that he relied on it for work.

"Go on, Nina, tell us the rest," Trent told her, obviously feeling just as impatient to learn the truth to her earlier statement. Had she almost killed the man? Was she on the run from police? Could this guy be searching for her right now?

"After I got sick, I ran to the bathroom. I could hear Rico yelling, cursing at the woman to leave and then cursing at me. He was raging about why I showed up."

"The dick's name is Rico?" Johnny asked.

She looked at him, swallowed hard as if she hadn't meant to reveal his name to them. She went on.

"Rico entered the bathroom as I was washing up. He started yelling at me. 'What the fuck, Nina?' he yelled and hit me. The backhand came so fast, so hard I fell to the left and hit my cheek on the porcelain bathtub. I was dazed from the hit and couldn't even comprehend that this was happening. Rico had always been gentle. Commanding and bossy, but gentle. Then suddenly he was pulling me by my hair, dragging me from the bathroom."

"Oh God," Johnny whispered. She stood up, walked across the room, her arms crossed in front of her chest. It was as if she were reliving the events. She stared off, not making eye contact with them, and all Buddy and his brothers could do was listen.

"I was never so scared, so frightened by a man's anger before. I somehow pushed him to his limit and he was the one who was caught cheating."

"No, Nina, he was wrong. He was turning it around on you because of that control," Trent told her.

She went on as if she didn't believe what Trent said. She still somehow felt at fault and that was because of the number this guy did on her. It pissed Buddy off big-time.

"I begged him to stop. 'Rico, please. Stop it, don't do this. What did I do?' I asked him, hoping, pleading that he would tell me. I had nothing without him. No one and nowhere to go.

"He carried on about me showing up at the apartment and not being at work. 'You're cheating on me?' I asked him.

"He cursed, told me this was his business not mine. That I was to do as he said, that he owned me. I tried to reason with him but it didn't matter. He was enraged. He said such terrible things to me," she whispered, tears rolling down her cheeks, her arms still crossed, and her head down in defeat.

"Like what?" Buddy found himself asking.

She looked up at him, the sadness and the pain of the memory upsetting her. She had really thought this guy loved her. "He said I was his regular lay. That there were others. I was so shocked. But still, I was attached to him and believed all those things he said, and I asked him what I did wrong to deserve this. I told him that I never cheated on him. He cursed at me and said I would never cheat on him, never kiss another man, never mind fuck another man because he would beat me and kill the guy."

"Bastard," Trent said and ran his fingers through his hair.

She went on telling the rest of the story. "I was angry and questioned him about Stacy, and how he could cheat but I was to stay faithful. I'll never forget that evil look in his eyes. The way he ate up my body, like he was determining where he would strike first. He yanked the belt from the waist of his pants and ran it over his palm as he spoke to me, threatened me, and then began to attack me."

"He hit you with the belt?" Johnny asked, sounding outraged and angry.

"Those are the scars on your back, and on your forearms?" Trent asked, his whisper a true show of his disgust. Buddy swallowed hard. Trent knew what it was like to have scars. Being burned in a fire set by an arsonist five years ago had left him with scars along his ribs and abdomen.

"What did you do?" Buddy asked.

"I begged for him to stop. I covered my face and my head from the strikes. He warned me, and told me that I was to keep quiet, to do as he said, and to never leave him. He said he could be with whomever he wanted to be with. That he could fuck one, two, three women together if he wanted to because he was the boss, the man. He struck me again, kicked me, and I begged for him to stop. I told him I would obey him. He finally stopped, fell to his knees, and grabbed me by my face. He was wild with anger." She took a few unsteady breaths, the tears stopped but her voice began to quiver with each new word she spoke.

"He said, 'You're mine. No other man will ever have you. This is your life now. I say when it's over.' I realized in that moment how stupid I was. How I was a bad judge of character, how I let my heart, my emotions make the decisions for me."

"It's not like that now, Nina. You know more, you've learned from this," Johnny said.

"I learned what? That any man is capable of that, of what he did? You don't understand, Johnny. You're not getting it. It didn't end there. I pushed him over the edge. I defied him and he was going to teach me a lesson I would never forget," she stated, raising her voice. She was shaking with emotion.

"Continue. Tell us what happened," Trent pushed. She looked at him, nibbled her bottom lip, and shook her head.

"Yes, tell us so we understand," Buddy added this time.

"It's too hard. It's embarrassing, and sick."

"We need to know everything, especially after you said you almost killed him," Trent reminded her.

She wiped a tear away from her eye before it fell. "He stared at me in disgust, but he was the one who did the damage. The bruised, cut cheek, bloody lip, cuts and marks all over my forearms and back. He broke the skin and it burned. And he had the nerve to tell me to tell him that I loved him."

Her lips were quivering. She was petrified as if it just happened to her now.

"I went to speak and he raised his hand at me, so I quickly said, 'I love you.'"

"What did he do?"

She stared at Trent and Buddy with a blank look in her eyes. "He told me that I needed to show him. Then he proceeded to order me to get undressed and get on the bed."

Buddy's eyes widened in shock.

Nina spoke faster. "I guess I didn't move fast enough for him. He pulled me up by my blouse, ripped it as he spoke with teeth clenched against my face. I don't remember what he said, just that he was so angry he shook me and told me that he was in charge, that I was going to learn the hard way and to do what he said or the punishments were going to get worse."

"Punishments? He hurt you before? He struck you before this incident?" Trent asked her.

"He was always possessive and handsy. I couldn't walk too far away from him because he would get angry if other men looked at me. But this statement, his threats, meant more. He was going to rape me. He was going to do god knows what to me to get his message across. He tore the blouse from my body and he struck me again and again and kept yelling. 'Get undressed. Take it all off.'"

Nina covered her ears and yelled out his words then cried and started rambling on as she clenched her fists and shook with emotion.

"He hit me so damn hard that I hit the side dresser. I grabbed onto the solid wood. I didn't want to die but I knew it could be that bad. That he was capable of such a thing and more. I saw a marble dolphin statue as he ripped my skirt, scratched my skin like some wild animal. The anger, the need to fight filled my belly. Then I felt the strikes from his belt again. He was hitting me over and over again against my back, and my ass. I felt it break my skin and I screamed out in pain and anger as he ripped the remainder of my clothing and I knew he was going to rape me. I was losing my hold of the dresser with every whip of the belt. I gripped the marble dolphin and used all my strength to pick up the thing and I swung it around me and I hit Rico just right. He fell to the ground, blood dripped from his skull, and he passed out. I was so scared, and I thought I had killed him. I carefully went closer. I heard him moan and made the decision to run, just grab what I could and run away as far as I could go so he could never find me. I even threw his cell phone in the toilet so he couldn't call his heavies to find me."

She was crying harder now and Johnny pulled her into his arms and held her tight. "It's okay, baby. You're safe now. We've got you."

She pushed away but he kept his hands on her hips. "No. No, Johnny, it's not over. I've been on the run for months. I thought I could settle down, but the truth is I can't live like this. I can't even apply for a new driver's license or open a checking account or do anything that could help them to find me."

"What makes you think he's still looking?" Trent asked, joining them, standing next to Johnny and her.

"Did you not hear what I told you? He's crazy. He's obsessed and he said I could never be with another man. He said that he owns me and he meant forever."

"You don't know if he's still looking for you."

"I know he is. No one defies Rico or ignores his orders without there being serious consequences. I tried to kill him. I wouldn't let him rape me and take what he wanted. He's going to look for me until he finds me. I know this man well. He never gives up, and one day he will succeed. That's why I can't get involved with any of you. I can't take that chance. He'll find me and he'll hurt or kill you."

* * * *

Trent was furious as he looked at Buddy. Then he looked at Johnny just as Nina was pushing away and trying to keep some distance between them.

"Nina, look at me," Trent said.

He knew that his brothers cared for her already. He knew he did as well. They had been hurt before. Hell, he had been with women who found his scars disgusting and they kept their eyes closed when they were having sex. He said he didn't care and thought it was a means to getting what he needed, but that was a lie. He understood about scars that ran deeper than the surface. He needed to protect his family, his brothers. He had to get proof about this guy.

She looked at him.

"Be honest now, are you attracted to the three of us? Did you feel as amazing as we did when we had the chance to kiss?"

Her eyes welled up with tears but none fell. She covered her mouth with her hand and started to shake it side to side but then closed her eyes and sobbed the word "yes."

"Give me his full name. This Rico guy."

Her eyes widened and she shook as she began steeping away from him. "No. No, Trent, what are you going to do?"

"I'm just going to see if he exists. If his club exists, and maybe if there were any reports of you missing, or his assault."

"Why are you doing this?" she asked, and then her mouth gaped open. "You don't believe me. You don't believe a word I said."

"That's not what he's saying and why he's asking. We're investigators," Buddy added.

"Investigating is one thing, but that's not what's happening here. You want more proof, yet you expect me to truly trust you, which I did and shared my entire fucked-up life with you and how this man used me, assaulted me, and then you do this?"

"We have our own hang-ups and insecurities when it comes to women and relationships, Nina," Trent told her.

"And this gives you more rights than me?"

"Trust me please. If things work out the way we hope, then I'll have an opportunity to explain it to you one day really soon," Trent added.

"Please, Nina. We can help," Johnny offered.

"We're not leaving you or going anywhere. We're right here," Buddy said, and Nina looked at the three of them.

Trent feared she might push them away entirely, but he had hope when she whispered, "Fine. But please don't let him find me."

Trent nodded and knew he would have to be extremely careful with this. He was going to need Jake. No one was going to hurt Nina ever again.

Chapter 6

"This guy, Rico Montero is a real piece of work, Buddy. You both need to check this out." Jake passed over a folder.

Trent opened it up, and it was Buddy who was shocked at the details.

"Fucking great. The FBI are investigating him?" Buddy asked. Jake nodded.

"Where did you get this information? How come they haven't arrested him yet?" Trent asked.

"I spoke with Turbo Hawkins," Jake said.

"Deputy Turbo Hawkins? What does he have to do with this?" Buddy asked.

"Turbo and Nate's brother, Rye, was involved with a special team of military soldiers for the government. Anyway, he's got some major connections in the federal government and ways of snooping around without raising red flags."

"Rye, who does handyman work and construction?" Buddy asked, sounding shocked.

Jake smirked and nodded his head. "You'd be surprised at what a lot of the residents of Treasure Town have been involved in and are capable of. So far so good, of course, but still."

"So what did he think of all this? What do we do?" Buddy asked.

"Well, Rye is currently trying to speak with an old military buddy of his to find out where they are in the investigation and if there are any updates. It seems the gambling thing is what the feds are really after. Rico runs multiple high-roller games in his club in the back room. Completely illegal of course, and it just so happens that a few people have disappeared after engaging in these illegal games."

"Someone is killing people?" Trent asked, rubbing his hand along his chin.

"Someone is ensuring that no one finds out about these dead people. But recently, some senator's son was involved in one of these things, a man with a bad habit, and he lost big. When he did, he didn't want to pay up and started talking about reporting Rico and the gambling operation, and getting away with the money he owed because of his father. Needless to say, the kid turned up dead that night after he left the club."

"Holy shit. So that's the only reason why the FBI are interested. This senator has been making a stink, I bet," Trent stated, sounding annoyed.

"Whatever, just as long as it puts the pressure on this Rico guy. Maybe they'll gather some evidence to prove he was part of those murders and he'll go away for a very long time. Nina would be safe then," Buddy told them.

"Yeah, well it doesn't seem like it will go that easy. Was Rye able to find out more from his friend about where they are in the investigation and an arrest?" Trent asked.

"He's working on it. They didn't want to snoop too much. Rye's connection will call in a day or so," Jake told them.

"Well, there's not much we can do right now but keep an eye on things around here," Buddy stated.

"And of course keep an extra eye on your woman, Nina." Jake smiled as he walked around his desk.

"Our woman?" Trent asked.

"Well, unless you'd like to set the record straight and say she's available? I can tell you for certain that the majority of the firefighters in Engine 20, never mind a good number around town, are interested in Nina. She's a gorgeous young woman."

"What the fuck?" Trent stated aloud and Jake laughed.

"Well, like I said, your woman."

Buddy took a deep breath and released it then looked at Jake.

"She has to accept us first, Jake. Nothing is concrete, and to tell you the truth, she's been avoiding us since explaining about her life, and refused to even get together to eat."

"She'll get over it, Buddy. It's your jobs, all three of you, to help her feel safe and know you can be trusted."

"I'm worried. Johnny said before all this, the other day, she nearly passed out," Buddy told him.

"Passed out? From what?"

"I thought it was heat stroke. When I saw her at the pizza place on the boardwalk a couple of weeks ago, she seemed overheated," Trent said.

"Nope. Johnny questioned her. He found out she had a granola bar for dinner the night before and nothing else all day. She needed the bike to go to the store but she also doesn't eat three meals a day. We think it's because she couldn't afford to."

"Damn, that's terrible. She really needs you guys," Jake added.

"Well, whether she wants to accept the help and the caring or not, she has no choice. We'll gain that trust eventually, but for now, she needs protection and men who can do just that," Trent said, and Buddy agreed. Jake shook their hands good-bye.

"I'll keep you posted. Go get her, Trent. Make her see that the Landers brothers are for real."

* * * *

"So you're avoiding them?" Cindy asked Nina after she dropped off an order of pies to Sullivan's.

"Well, it's easier this way," Nina said, sitting down and crossing her legs. She looked tired and thinner than just a few days ago.

Cindy reached over and covered her hand, giving it a gentle squeeze. Nina jerked but didn't pull away as they locked gazes.

"When was the last time you ate?" she asked her.

Nina's cheeks turned a nice shade of red. "Just a little while ago?"

Cindy pulled away, feeling annoyed that Nina for lying. She crossed her arms and gave her a mean look. "You're such a liar."

"Liar?"

"Yeah, you suck at lying. It's written all over your face. Why aren't you eating? You're making good money, the Landers brothers aren't even charging you rent. You're still wearing the same four outfits you've been wearing since you got into town. Don't you think it's time for a change?"

Nina shrugged her shoulders. "I have a lot on my mind."

"The three brothers?" Cindy asked. Nina went to speak and Cindy held up her hand. "Please don't even try it, girl. You like them."

"What's not to like? They're perfect."

"They like you, so what's the problem?"

"A lot of things."

"Like what?"

"Please, Cindy. I don't want to talk about it."

"A guy from your past did you wrong and now you think all men are the same?"

Nina shot her head up, eyes wide, mouth gaped open. Cindy nodded.

"I think we can start a club around Treasure Town with other women just like us."

"This is different."

"How so?"

"Well, like I said. I don't want to talk about it."

"Well, you can't let the past and some asshole ruin your future and your happiness. Take it from me, I know firsthand. My ex was a real piece of work. I had to sneak out of town before he could catch me."

"What?"

"Well, the fact that I stole five thousand dollars out of his not-so-secret hiding spot in his apartment might be why he probably would like to wring my neck. But, it's been two years, so I'd say he's moved on with some bimbo and more than likely not the one I caught him in bed with."

"Oh no. The same thing sort of happened to me." Nina started to explain a little bit about her ex and how things went down. Cindy got the gist of it.

"You should meet Tasha and Michaela. They both went through some crazy stuff. Tasha was forced to work under cover for the federal government and date a man who killed her father. She nearly lost Eddie, Lance, and Tyler Martelli."

"Oh my God, that sounds so intense. Wait, Martelli? Why does that sound familiar?"

"Oh, you probably met their father, the fire chief for Engine 19 when your apartment was on fire. As a matter of fact, Ace and Bull were two of the firefighters there."

"My, this really is a close-knit town. Everyone seems to know everyone."

"I told you it's a great place. I was on the road for a while when I came across Treasure Town. That was two years ago, and I don't plan on leaving here. Besides, the prospects in the male department are pretty damn awesome."

Nina looked around them and then stared back at the table. "I don't think I'll ever feel confident enough to date anyone or let them get close."

Cindy touched her hand. "Hey, in time you'll heal from whatever that ex of yours did to you. You'll get stronger, especially if you take care of your body and eat well."

"Okay, I'll work on that."

"You'd better."

"Well, I'd better head back to the apartment before the guys get home from work."

"Oh, they have you on a curfew or do you have a hot date with them?" Cindy teased.

Nina widened her eyes. "Neither. Of course neither. I just want to get there and be inside before they get home. I told you, avoiding them is easier and safer than facing them right now."

"You won't be able to avoid them for long. All three of them are pretty stubborn and bossy men. They're used to giving orders, organizing investigations, and have amazing reputations. Johnny is probably the most easygoing of the three and he's so damn adorable. How can you resist those big muscular arms and sexy blue eyes? I could just eat him up."

Nina looked away and then whispered to Cindy, "If you like him, you can ask him out."

"Are you out of your mind? He wants you. Gosh, Nina, I don't think you shared enough information about your ex. I can tell he must have weakened your self-esteem. We need to get that back."

"Get it back?"

"Yes. I think I have an idea. Can I pick you up tomorrow at noon?"

"Sure. I only have tomorrow off and then I have more orders to bake."

"Cool. I'll see you then. Oh, do you need me to call one of the guys to come get you?"

"No," Nina said and looked at Cindy like she had two heads.

Cindy laughed. "I was just messing with ya. But don't be surprised if your little trick doesn't work with avoiding them. They're detectives after all."

"Wonderful."

* * * *

As Nina rode her bike back toward the apartment, she thought about the guys. Cindy was right. Johnny had the most amazing blue eyes and adorable face. He was muscular, yet kind of reminded her of a buffed-out Tom Cruise. She laughed at that. Many probably flirted with him like crazy and especially on calls with work. Damsels in distress. That was something she didn't want to be to them.

He was definitely the most compassionate out of the three. It was he who offered their apartment for free to her, a perfect stranger.

Then there was Buddy Landers. Boy could that man stop traffic with his looks and his muscular body. He was sexy, tall, and had dark hair that somehow made his blue eyes stand out. She couldn't help but stare at him in awe. He was that handsome. But he had a way about him. Tough, bossy, and charismatic were pretty good words to describe Buddy.

Then there was Trent. That man gave her palpitations from his authoritative, "guilty before proven innocent" expression every time their eyes locked. She couldn't help but to feel that Trent trusted her the least and, like her, had difficulty opening up his heart.

As she got closer to the street before the driveway to their house, she heard a truck approaching. She looked over her shoulder to see who it was, hoping that it wasn't Buddy, Trent, and Johnny before she could get inside her apartment and hide. It was Trent. She turned around a little too quickly and lost her footing. Her balance went next as the handlebars shook and she rode over the gravel on the side of the road and into a rut. In a flash she was on her side, elbow burning and ass stinging.

She heard the tires squeal as she tried to unwrap herself from the bike.

"Nina, my God, are you okay?" Buddy asked.

She looked up to see Trent and Buddy. Buddy got to her first. He carefully pulled the bike out of the way, tossing it to the side. Nina tried to stand up, but the second she moved, her ass and back hurt.

"Ouch."

"Whoa, slow down. You're hurt."

When Buddy reached out and touched her cheek, she froze in place. They locked gazes.

"Let me help you."

She stared at him until her elbow began to throb something terrible.

"I can get up," she said, but in her position she couldn't. Buddy reached down and lifted her by her waist. She wound up against his chest on the side of the road, and before he lost his balance, he hoisted her in the air and stepped toward the truck.

She straddled his waist. "What are you doing?

"Looking over the damage. Come on now and sit down on the bed of the truck."

Trent pulled the back tailgate down and Buddy placed her on it. She cringed and ran her hand to her ass and tried rubbing it where it hurt. It was her lower back and butt that ached. She felt like she was bleeding.

Trent walked over with a first aid kit as Buddy ran the palms of his hands on her thighs. "Where does it hurt the most?" he asked. But she couldn't concentrate. Not with his large hands rubbing up and down her thighs.

"Her elbow is bleeding. Let's get this bandaged up and then take her back to the house to look her over better," Trent said.

Buddy held her arm and looked at the damage. "We should really wash this out first."

"I'll wrap this gauze around it for now but when we get to the house we'll clean it out good."

"That's okay. I can do it myself. Johnny gave me that kit."

Trent ignored her and wrapped the elbow with the gauze. Then Buddy gently raised her arm and leaned down to kiss her bandage.

"What are you doing?" she asked in shock pulling away.

"Kissing it to make it better. Did it work?" he asked her teasingly.

She felt her cheeks warm, and her body was suddenly overheated. Why whenever these men were around did her pussy leak cream and her nipples actually harden? Was this even normal?

She tried to slide down off the truck but Buddy caught her. He helped her down, slowly, letting his body rub up against hers. The feel of steel-solid muscles aroused every part of her. She was overwhelmed at her response, even her throat felt as if it had closed up and she could barely breathe, panting instead.

"We'll bring you home. Come on, honey," Trent said. She heard his voice, it felt like little vibrations of desire traveled over her from Trent's voice alone. She held Buddy's gaze, mesmerized by his expression. A firm hand guided her toward the passenger side of the truck and before she could climb in, ass aching, Buddy lifted her up. She gasped and gripped his shirt.

"You're hurt. As soon as we get you to our place, we're going to look you over. Thoroughly."

All she could do was gulp. Buddy was an extremely macho, tough man. He had this look in his eyes all the time. Same with Trent. It was like they were a force to reckon with, but not in a bad way, more like for the good guys.

She felt as if that thought was rather delusional. Was she thinking positive thoughts in order to condone her body's reaction to these men? Was she simply looking for excuses to try and open up her heart one more time? Fear gripped her insides as she prayed she didn't get sick.

Every time she felt something meaningful directly to her core and her heart, thoughts of Rico and her past invaded and destroyed those thoughts. Would she ever feel safe, confident, and willing to risk a broken heart or even a broken body? Why did thoughts of being with any man make her feel pain, worthlessness, and like she was being used?

She closed her eyes to will back the tears and adjusted her body in the seat. Both men climbed into the truck and she felt claustrophobic.

She zoned in on her aching elbow and her sore ass and hip to clear her head of the lustful, wanting thoughts now ruling her mind.

This was not real. Their desire for her, their attraction, their compassion was an act. They would hurt her threefold. They were even bigger than Rico, more capable than Rico, and they would destroy her once and for all.

* * * *

Buddy's heart was hammering in his chest. He couldn't believe how turned on and aroused her was. When he saw Nina riding her bike, her ass moving on the small bike seat and her toned thighs accentuated with every stroke of the pedal when she pushed down, it aroused him. She was wearing a black tank top and flimsy cotton shorts that hugged the curves of her ass. The tank lifted slightly, revealing toned abs and tan skin. But when she looked back, the shocked expression on her face, and look of intimidation did something to him. When she lost control of the bike and fell, he cursed, as did his brother Trent, who stepped on the gas and quickly pulled over.

She was not going to ignore them and hide from them any longer. Seeing her injured did something to his insides. It upset him, angered him, and made him want to wrap her up in his arms and protect her from ever feeling any pain even as minor as a bee sting ever again.

As Trent pulled into the long driveway, they both saw Johnny's truck, and he smiled to himself. Johnny must have headed home early to try to catch Nina before she got to her apartment. It seemed even Johnny was getting fed up with Nina hiding out and avoiding them.

"We'll get you patched up quickly, especially with Johnny here. He'll make sure you didn't get hurt worse than you're letting on," Trent told her firmly and Buddy felt her leg shaking. She was nervous.

"I told you that I'm okay. I can take care of myself."

"No you can't. That's why we're here," Trent snapped at her.

The truck stopped and Buddy got out then reached for Nina.

"I can do it," she said, holding his gaze, but damn it, he needed to touch her again, to feel her in his arms. Wanting her acceptance was becoming a priority.

"I'm going to carry you and you're going to let me." He pulled her by her hips toward him. Her thighs widened as she slipped on the leather seats and wound up straddling Buddy's waist. He stood there holding her hips, and she placed her hands on his shoulders for support.

Gazes locked, heart racing, he spoke softly to her. "You are the most gorgeous woman I have ever laid eyes on. I'll admit, I've known a lot of women in my thirty-two years of life, but none, and I mean none whatsoever, compare to you, Nina. I want to help you. I want to protect you, wrap you in my arms and take away that expression of fear, timidity, and uncertainty that some asshole caused. Now, I'm not the only one who feels this way. Avoiding us isn't going to happen anymore. I'm carrying you inside our house. We're going to make sure you're okay, and maybe, maybe I'll even kiss each boo-boo, and you're going to let me because you want to and you feel the attraction, too. Now, hold on, honey, while I carry you."

He felt her hands grip his shoulders and then she hugged him as he carried her into the house.

Buddy locked gazes with Trent who winked and opened the door for them.

As he carried her into the kitchen he saw Johnny standing there, concern filled his eyes.

Buddy was too consumed with emotions, feeling Nina cling to him as he placed her ass down on the island in the kitchen. She didn't let go. Instead she hugged him tighter and he knew his words, his confession and honesty, had gotten to her.

He rubbed her back as Johnny and Trent stood on either side of her.

"It's okay, baby. My brothers feel the same way and want the same thing. To protect you and get to know you better. You feel so good in my arms." He whispered on the top of her head and then kissed her hair. Her fingers tightened and he could feel her warm breath penetrate his shirt over his heart.

"What happened? Why the bandage?" Johnny asked, and Trent explained. Nina slowly pulled back and her expression of uncertainty pulled at Buddy's heartstrings. Her lips were wet and full, her eyes glossy, and having her this close to him, with her breasts nearly pouring from the tank top, was too much to resist.

"I'm going to kiss you now, Nina, and you're going to let me because you want to, don't you, honey?" he asked. Her cheeks turned a shade redder, but he wanted to leap for joy when she nodded her head in compliance.

He leaned closer and took her lips gently, to savor in the taste, the feel of such a sweet, intimate action. Her palms rubbed his chest and he pulled her closer, ran his large hands over her delicate, feminine back then up under her hair to the base of her neck. He plunged his tongue deeper, and ravaged her mouth, unable to stop himself from wanting more.

He pulled her closer with his other arm wrapped around her and now her breasts were pressed against his chest, her warm pussy could be felt against his skin despite the material that covered his belly. She began to move against him and he wanted nothing more than to bury his cock deep inside of her and make her part of him and him a part of her forever.

He moved his lips along her cheeks and neck as she tilted her head back, giving him access to her body. He cupped her breast and she moaned.

"Oh God, Buddy, I can't believe this. I never felt anything like this before."

"That's because this is real. Our feelings for you, our desire to protect you and make you all ours is real," Trent told her and Buddy massaged her left breast, completely turned on that it didn't fit in his large hands.

"You're perfect and so beautiful, Nina," Johnny told her as he placed his hand against her cheek and kissed her deeply.

Buddy pulled her off the counter while Johnny continued to kiss her and then Trent joined in. The second Trent touched her, ran his hands under her tank top against her skin, she moaned into Johnny's mouth.

Her hips were moving and Buddy was pressing his cock against her crotch as Trent was rocking his hips slowly against her ass. Buddy imagined them taking her together, filling her in every hole, and bringing her more pleasure than she ever experienced in her life.

Johnny pulled from her mouth, breathing heavy, and Trent lifted her tank top up and over her head.

She gasped and pulled back only for Trent to turn her face toward him and tell her how he felt.

"You are an amazing woman. We're not going to hurt you. In fact we want to bring you pleasure and make you part of us, Nina. Let go of the fear and give us this chance to show you, to prove that the four of us can be one, can be a family."

"Family?" she asked, her voice cracking.

"Damn straight. You're everything we've ever wanted in a woman for the three of us. Please, Nina, let go, and let us in," Johnny begged.

* * * *

Nina was shaking with desire and, of course, fear. This was a chance she thought she wasn't willing to take. She never wanted to feel hurt, betrayed, or used again. She never imagined being involved in such an unconventional relationship as a ménage, yet here she was considering it. She knew if she said yes and she allowed them to make love to her, then she would truly be ruined forever. There would be no other man, or men, in her life, in her bed, inside of her but these three men.

"Nina?" Trent whispered as he kissed her neck and then her shoulders and back.

"I'm scared," she admitted, holding Johnny's gaze.

"So am I. I'm afraid you'll continue to push us away, or you'll leave us and not be able to commit to the three of as we make a commitment to you. It scares me to take this chance, yet I've never felt so compelled, so right about anyone like I do about you with us."

"We'll go as slow as you need, Nina," Buddy told her.

She swallowed the lump of fear and emotion in her throat. She loved how their hands felt on her, against her skin. She wasn't even freaking out that Trent had a perfect view of her back and the faint scars along it. She just knew that she felt content and safe this close to these three men.

"Nina?" Buddy whispered.

"Kiss me, Buddy. Just keep making me feel important, special, and cared for. It's all I ask right now. It's more than anyone has ever given to me."

* * * *

Buddy felt so bad for her. To know that no one had ever shown her true love and compassion was heart wrenching. He would make it his mission in life to always make her feel special and a part of him, starting today.

He leaned forward and kissed her deeply, explored her mouth, and swallowed her moans of pleasure as he moaned along with her. He wanted to explore every inch of her body, and as he reached back to unclip her bra, she pulled back and stared at him. He took his time. His brothers stood beside him as the black lace bra fell to her shoulders and the sight of her gorgeous, sexy breasts came into view.

Nina licked her lips and took a deep breath. He wondered if she would stop here and not go any further. He didn't even care right now. Any part of her she was willing to give was a step closer to making her theirs.

She shocked them when she removed the bra the rest of the way, ran her hands up his chest, and kissed him.

He hugged her to him, feeling this petite, sexy woman in his arms as he wrapped her up just like he wanted to and carried her upstairs to the master bedroom.

* * * *

Nina stood there in the bedroom, half-naked, and Buddy and Johnny spoke softly to her. They told her how lovely her breasts were, how soft her skin felt, but Trent focused on her back and her ass and the faint lines of scarring that remained there. Johnny was pushing her shorts down as Buddy removed his shirt, and Nina reached out to press her palm against his skin. Buddy closed his eyes and held her wrist then moved her hand down lower to his cock over his dress pants.

Trent took in the sight of her faint scars, the ones on her ass a little darker in comparison to her back. He reached out and ran a finger gently over the marks, he leaned forward and kissed them when Nina tightened up and looked over her shoulder at Trent.

"Please don't look."

He held her gaze, ran his finger along her chin and jaw, and looked deep within her eyes. "You're not the only one with scars, baby. I know exactly how you feel, and how much deeper these go than the surface."

"How?" she asked, her eyes glazed over with unshed tears.

He stepped back slightly and pulled his shirt up and over his head.

He knew the second she saw the burn marks, the scarring from the fire. It ran along his ribs and toward his lower back. She inhaled and then locked gazes with him. In that moment Trent felt as if they connected on such a deep level it frightened him and left him in awe. He didn't think he could feel more compelled to love her until she lowered onto her knees, ran her hands along the scarring, then softly brushed her lips against the raised skin.

He closed his eyes and ran his fingers through her hair while she hugged him around his center.

Overwhelmed by the connection and the emotions he felt, he lifted her up and kissed her deeply, as he used his hands to explore her naked, curvy body. He squeezed her ass and she thrust against his hips.

He lifted her up and carried her to the bed.

When he laid Nina down, she looked like a goddess. Her long brown locks cascaded over the comforter. Her mocha eyes held his with a mix of anticipation and arousal. He wanted this to be perfect.

"Slow, Nina. Nice and slow," he whispered, trailing his fingers along her jaw, down her throat, over her taut belly, and to her mound. Her eyes darted to either side of him, and he knew that Buddy and Johnny were there, undressing, revealing their bodies to her and what would soon be hers.

Trent leaned over with his thigh between her thighs, and he softly kissed her lips. He slowly, gently kissed a trail along her skin exploring her breasts, licking and swirling his tongue around her areola as she moaned and shook beneath him.

"You taste so sweet, Nina. As sweet as those delicious pies you make."

His brother Buddy crawled up on the right side of her and began to explore her breasts. He kissed Nina on the lips and then along her breast and areola as Trent made his way with his mouth and hands between her thighs.

The moment his thumbs touched her groin, she tightened up.

Johnny was there to calm her fears as he lay down to the left of her. He cupped her cheek so she would look at him.

"Easy, baby, we're going to take this nice and slow so you know how much you already mean to all three of us. If we do something that scares you, makes you feel afraid or uncomfortable, you let us know, and we'll stop." Her eyes widened and Trent paused.

"You'd do that? You'd stop for me?"

Trent needed to shove down his anger at the bastard who hurt her so deeply she feared that the only way to take a woman was roughly and without her consent. If he ever got the chance to meet the fucker, he would be sure to teach him a lesson about how to treat a woman.

"Of course we will. We're not him, Nina. Remember that you can trust us," Buddy told her.

Trent lowered to his knees by the bed and stroked his thumbs along her pussy lips. She jerked and then tightened up, prepared to pull her legs closed, but he was between them. Buddy and Johnny slowly pushed their palms onto her thighs, keeping her wide open for them. He wasn't sure what her reaction might be as he paused to feel her out when she moaned, closed her eyes, and cream dripped from her cunt.

"Damn, baby, you are so responsive and sexy. I love it," Trent said and leaned forward to take a taste.

Nina quivered beneath him, but with every stroke of his tongue, every nip to her clit, her body showed her enjoyment, and her moans turned to soft mews of pleasure.

"So delicious. My brothers are going to love how you taste, baby." Trent maneuvered a finger to her cunt and slowly pressed his digit up into her. He watched how her pussy gripped it tight and drew it in as she thrust her hips upward.

"Will you let us make love to you, sweetie?" he asked her.

She opened her arms and held his gaze.

"Come closer," she whispered with tears in her eyes. His heart raced. It ached with emotion.

He leaned up and she placed her palms against his cheeks and held his gaze.

"I'm so scared right now. But, all three of you touching me, saying the things that you're saying to me, is making me want to try this with you. I want to feel more. I want to be free of him, Trent. Free of the past, the pain, and the fear. I don't ever want to feel used, abandoned, and alone again. Is it a mistake? Will I regret this, or will I regret turning the three of you away and never knowing what it feels like to actually have men care about me?"

Trent turned his face slightly and kissed her palm. Johnny kissed her left shoulder and Buddy kissed her right.

"We know that you're scared," Trent said. "We've all made mistakes, made poor choices or may have been involved in things we're ashamed of or things that changed how we feel about connecting to other people or even opening up our hearts to love. I can tell you that I haven't been with a woman in quite some time because of my fears, my insecurities about my scars. I'm not saying that I was a saint, Nina. God knows I've fucked around just to feel anything instead of feeling empty. But with you, being here with you like this is so damn amazing. Ask my brothers and they'll tell you this is real, and this is special."

She looked at Buddy. "You are the most amazing woman we've ever met. I know I've never met a woman who struck me so deeply so instantly like you did when we first met. You're a grown woman, Nina. You're not a kid, you've had to go through some pretty dangerous and serious things in your life to get here, and to break free. That takes a mind, a determination, and a desire to be someone. This decision is all yours, and if you say you need to wait out of fear that we could hurt you or that you may regret it, then hell, baby, we'll wait. It will be fucking torture, but you're worth it."

He winked and Nina nodded.

"Your choice, Nina," Johnny said. "We'll wait for you. We've waited this long to find a woman who could complete our family and make us feel so deeply it actually hurts inside. You're ours and we're yours."

* * * *

Nina took a few unsteady breaths as their words filtered through her head. They were already so different than what she was used to men being like. They were compassionate, loving, and affectionate and put her first even before their needs. She could feel Trent's erection against her mound. To know that he would stop things right now, all three of them would put their needs aside and allow her time to ease into this, touched her heart.

Their bodies were so amazing, and she wanted to feel them against her and feel their cocks inside of her, joining their bodies as one. Trent shared her fears, her insecurities about the scars because he had scars, too. All of this talking, touching, exploring made her feel so comfortable that she knew she wanted to take a chance. If it turned to shit, then so be it. At least they had tonight. They had one another.

"I want to try. I want to feel all three of you kissing me, touching me, and making me feel beautiful."

"You already are beautiful," Johnny said and leaned down to kiss her shoulder. His mouth continued to explore her skin then trail down over her breast. She was shocked when Buddy did the same on her other side to her other breast just as Johnny nipped her nipple.

"Oh." She moaned.

"I'll grab the condoms and the lube," Trent whispered, kissing along her belly and between her thighs.

"You don't need any condoms. I'm covered," she told him, thinking of the IUD she had gotten when she first met Rico. Although she never told him and made him use a condom, she was glad now. Knowing he was unfaithful, she was glad she took precautions to protect herself from any diseases.

Trent smiled as he removed his pants. She saw the scars, the remnants of an injury she yearned to hear about. She yearned to understand his turmoil like he understood hers.

Trent eased up between her legs and kissed her lips. "You ready for me, baby?" he asked her and she smiled.

"Ready." She tilted her chin up to lick under his chin, his neck, then back up to his lips. He leaned lower and she kissed him as he eased his cock up into her needy cunt. He grunted and tried to push through, but she was tight. She could feel him struggling. He released her lips.

"Damn, woman, you're tight." He eased out a little and then thrust back into her all the way. She moaned and he held himself within her, panting.

"So good. You feel so tight and warm. Holy shit, I am not going to last. You're mine now, Nina. Mine." He began a series of faster thrusts in and out of her pussy. Nina held on to his shoulders, ran her hands along his biceps, and then back to his cheeks. She held his face between her palms and absorbed the struggling expression, as if he were holding back or truly feeling overwhelmed by the muscles in her cunt gripping his cock.

It made her feel sexy, appealing, and enticing like some erotic goddess, and she pumped upward.

"Oh fuck," he said against her neck and reached under her to spread her ass cheeks wide as he pulled her nearly off the bed and began to thrust deeper, faster. The bed rocked, they both moaned, and she felt the orgasm coming closer and closer. Her ass ached, her hips a little sore from her fall, and he thrust into her to the hilt.

"Oh God, Trent, faster, harder please."

"Fuck, baby, you look so fucking hot," Johnny said from the side. It seemed to set Trent off as he lifted up, pulling her thighs higher, spreading her ass cheeks wider while he rotated his hips and stroked as deeply and quickly as he could. Her breasts were shaking and her belly was tight when she felt his cock grow thicker. She screamed her release. Trent followed, pumping one, two, three times and exploding inside of her.

"Nina!" he roared and kissed her on the mouth as she wrapped her arms around his neck and held on tight.

She never felt so loved, and so complete before. She was in love and the thought scared the crap out of her.

* * * *

Holy God, I love her. I can't believe this but I love Nina.

Trent squeezed her tight, felt the curves of her body beneath his palms, and he wanted nothing more than to continue to hold her, absorb her scent, her shampoo, and the feeling of completion with her in his arms. It frightened him to feel such strong emotions so quickly and deeply, but he did.

He knew his brothers waited for their turn. He looked at Buddy, who was stroking his cock, and Nina, who stared right at it.

"Are you okay?" Trent asked her.

She placed her palm against his cheek. "Better than okay." He smiled and then eased out of her and Buddy took his place.

* * * *

Buddy's cock was as hard as a fucking steel rod right now. Watching Trent make love to their woman was magical. She really was taking a huge risk by letting them love her, and he respected her and the decision. As aroused and needy as he felt right now, he knew that when the three of them made love to Nina together it would blow anything they ever fantasized about out of the water.

Buddy leaned up and kissed her lips.

"You've got me so very hard, Nina. Watching you make love to Trent was amazing, just like you're amazing."

"Thank you for taking your time with me. I need it like this. Slow, meaningful," she said. She looked like she still feared it may not be so meaningful or that she couldn't trust them fully. He knew it would take time. Time to heal from the past and the damage that guy had done to her. But he was feeling pretty damn possessive of Nina right now. He wanted to prove how meaningful this all really was.

He brushed her hair aside to hold her cheeks as he lay halfway over her. Just having the skin-to-skin contact and feeling her femininity, pressed tight underneath him, turned him on and surged his ego. She was their woman now. No other men would ever get to love her, hold her, and make her smile.

"I love your eyes, Nina. They're so different and attractive. They show your emotion, your fears and uncertainty even now as I lay here ready to love you next. I don't think you realize how special you already are to us. I can't wait to be inside of you, and when my brothers and I take you together, I hope you'll feel how special this bond between us really is."

"Together?" she asked, sounding concerned.

He eased up and kissed along her collarbone and her neck, making his way lower.

"Oh yes, Nina, together. Me inside this tight little wet pussy." He licked across her nipple as he used his finger to swipe up into her cunt.

"Oh."

"And me, with my cock inside of that sweet mouth of yours," Johnny chimed in.

"And me in that sexy ass I've been admiring for weeks now," Trent added.

"Oh God." She moaned.

"Hell, I can't hold off. Not this first time."

Buddy lifted up, aligned his cock with her pussy, and eased into her. Nina held on to his shoulders tilted her head back and came. She fucking came and he was inside of her for two strokes. It fed his ego, made him feel like a man, a superior lover, to do that to her. He gripped her hips and stroked into her fast.

Nina held on and tried to counterthrust but it was too much, the sight of her breasts moving with every thrust, her eyes holding his gaze as he clenched his teeth and tried relentlessly to ease the itch, the desire building and building within his cock. He thought he might really explode he felt so full and tight and ready to detonate. Nina caressed his chest, and he eased her lower on the bed, reaching underneath them and stroking a finger over her anus.

"Oh." She moaned again, the sloshing sound filled the room, and he stroked a finger over her cream then back to her anus and pressed inside of her. Nina shook and moaned deeply and Buddy lost it. One, two, three full, deep strokes and he held himself within her when he came, shooting his seed deeply and imagining her living in their house, sharing their bed forever.

"You're mine, Nina. Always." He kissed her swiftly and then hugged her to him as he rolled to the side, taking her along with him.

* * * *

Johnny moved in behind Nina as Buddy eased himself out of her. Johnny kissed along her shoulder and he was pleasantly surprised when she turned, lifted up, and climbed over him.

She sat up, her hands on his shoulders, and looked down into his eyes.

"Hi," she whispered.

"Hi," he replied, absorbing the sight of her full breasts and all the love marks along her neck and chest.

He reached up under her hair and drew her down closer for a kiss. She twirled her tongue around his mouth and they battled for control until she jerked.

He released her lips and Nina moaned.

Johnny chuckled. "What is Trent doing to you, baby?"

She eased up and moaned again. "Oh God."

"You ever have a cock in your ass, Nina?" Trent asked her as he gripped her hips. It appeared to Johnny that he licked along her spine as he pressed his fingers into her ass.

"No. Never."

Johnny's heart raced.

"Ever have a dick in your pussy, one in your mouth, and one in your ass at the same time?" Buddy asked, stroking his cock. Johnny knew why. They were going to take her together. His cock hardened beneath her.

She shook her head side to side as she moaned. Johnny lifted her up, aligned his cock to her cunt, and before he could tell her to ease down, Nina did it herself.

"Oh, Johnny." She moaned out his name as she sunk onto his shaft, taking him inside of her. Johnny tightened up, gripped her hips, and grunted as her pussy muscles gripped his cock.

"Holy shit, you're so tight, Nina. So fucking tight."

"She sure is, and we're going to ease some more lube in this ass and take her together. You're going to belong to us fully and see that this is real. We're real," Trent said, leading the way.

Johnny began to thrust up into Nina and she gripped his shoulders then tried to counterthrust. Buddy moved to the other side of the bed and held his cock in his hand.

"Sweet Nina, I need that mouth."

"Oh God, this is so crazy. I feel so crazy, wild, and naughty all at once."

Johnny held her neck and face so she would look at him. "It's time to get crazy, wild, and naughty with us, your men. Now be a good girl and suck Buddy's cock while Trent gets your ass ready for his cock."

He pulled her down as her eyes lit up, and he kissed her shocked expression from her face. He swirled his tongue in her mouth and then thrust upward with his cock, scraping her vaginal muscles.

When he released her, she looked so wanton and wild.

Buddy gripped her hair gently and guided her mouth to his cock. "Ready for you, baby. Nice and easy, you set the pace."

She licked the tip and Johnny saw Buddy's cock twitch, heard his brother grunt but hold steady. Johnny thrust upward and Nina opened her mouth and took Buddy deeper.

* * * *

Nina couldn't believe how she felt right now. Nothing ever made her feel like she belonged, like she was important and special the way making love to these three men did. She tried to keep up with Johnny's thrusts, but then she was focusing on sucking Buddy's cock and wanting to satisfy him, make him happy and make him come inside of her mouth so she could swallow his seed and let him know how special he was to her. All three men had ahold of her heart and she wanted to ride this out, enjoy every moment, and live like there was no tomorrow.

She felt Trent pull his fingers from her ass and she gasped with Buddy's cock in her mouth only to moan when she felt the tip of Trent's cock push into her anus. His hands were everywhere, caressing and massaging her skin. He had licked and kissed along her scars and she loved him for it. They made her feel so important, but now with a cock in every hole and her body about to lose it, she knew there was never going to be anything as amazing and powerful as these three men making love to her together. She would be ruined after today, and she didn't care. Instead she focused on them, this connection and the hope that nothing could tear them apart.

"Fuck, baby, I love this ass. This is my ass, Nina." Trent squeezed her cheeks wider and thrust into her deeply. Johnny was pumping his cock in and out of her cunt while she was trying to keep the same pace sucking down Buddy. Buddy gripped her hair and held himself within her as he came. He tried pulling back but she grabbed his thigh and held him against her, which earned her a caress along her hip from Trent and a squeeze of her breast from Johnny.

Buddy slowly pulled from her mouth and fell back onto the bed. She looked down at Johnny and both he and Trent began a fast pace, pumping into her together. Her arms were shaking. Her legs were, too, when suddenly she exploded, her cream causing both men to penetrate even deeper.

"Oh yeah, Nina. Come for us, baby. Keep coming. Give us all your orgasms," Trent ordered. She moaned and thrust on top, then felt tinier spasms hit her insides. Her pussy erupted again, and then Buddy leaned over as she sat up and he cupped her breast then stuck his tongue out to lick her nipple then suckled part of her breast into his mouth. The sensation of him pulling the sensitive bud between his teeth while Johnny and Trent continued their strokes made her moan aloud. It was all too much for her.

"Oh!" she cried out and orgasmed again.

"Oh God." Johnny grunted and thrust upward, held himself within her, and shook as he came. Behind her Trent held on to her hips and ground his cock deeper, faster into her ass. She felt the smack to her backside as he lowered her down onto Johnny, spread her thighs wider, and thrust into her again and again.

"Oh, Trent. I can't take it."

"Fuck, I love this ass." Trent moaned and then came, shooting his seed into her and rocking three more times before he stopped. She felt her ears ringing, her breathing was shallow, and she laid her cheek against Johnny's chest as he caressed her back and recovered as well.

"So incredible. Damn," Buddy said. Then she felt his hands caressing her ass and her back as Trent eased out of her.

"Mm." She moaned.

Then she felt Trent's lips along her lower back and her ass. "Rest, baby. Rest."

She closed her eyes and relished in the aftermath of some serious lovemaking by the three sexiest, most compassionate men she'd ever met.

Chapter 7

As Nina finished cleaning up the kitchen from baking her last pie, she thought about Trent, Johnny, and Buddy again. No matter where her thoughts wandered off to, even negative ones, she kept coming back to them. Last night was amazing and this morning? Incredible. They didn't want her to leave their house, never mind their bed, but she needed to make these pies to fill this order and she also needed a little breather. She had been worried about being clingy or possessive of them and overstaying her welcome, but then Johnny was talking about moving her things into their house and using their industrial oven to cook the pies and how there would be more room.

She couldn't help but feel tickled at his approach to saying he wanted to spend every waking hour he could with her. Instead she figured she wanted to do this right this time. She needed time to get to know them individually. Although she technically was already doing this backward by sleeping with them and allowing all three brothers to take her at once. She shrugged her shoulders.

Like I care. I don't regret a single moment. Except maybe falling on my ass and hip. Damn, I think I'm all bruised up from that.

She thought about how Johnny cleaned out the cut on her elbow and how his process of determining if she was indeed okay and not in need of further medical attention led to him taking her from behind while she sucked Trent's cock.

She shivered and her nipples hardened.

Great, now I'm horny again.

She bent down to pick up the box and felt the ache to her hip and butt. "Ouch." She rubbed it and tried turning sideways as far as she could to see if there was some bruising. She pressed her shorts down and lifted her tank top up.

"Whatever you're doing, can I help?"

She gasped as she heard the voice, turned toward the open door, and saw Buddy standing there behind the screen door. He opened it up and walked inside.

"Damn, it smells good in here. I wonder what it is." He approached and pulled her into his arms. She held onto his forearms and giggled as he sniffed against her neck, tickling her. That led to his hand under her shorts caressing her ass and his other hand under her tank top cupping her breast. He kissed her deeply and she softened in his embrace. When he finally released her lips, her eyes were closed and she felt like putty in them. "I missed you," he told her.

"I missed you, too," she replied and then tried standing straighter only for her hip to hit the counter. She cringed.

Buddy's eyes darkened and his eyebrows scrunched together before he stepped back. "What's wrong? Something hurts?" he asked with his hand on her waist.

She locked gazes with him. He really did care about her. He told her he never wanted her to feel any pain and she thought it was the sweetest thing, yet completely unrealistic.

"I think it's from the fall yesterday. I'm not sure if it's bruised."

"Let me see. I hope we weren't too rough with you for our first time together," he said and she gulped.

"Don't be silly, Buddy. That was incredible."

"But you're a petite little thing and not used to such big men like us taking you at once. Maybe we should have waited." He lifted her tank top and pulled on the elastic to her shorts, pressing the material down.

"No, Buddy. Don't say that. It was wonderful."

"Damn, this is bruised good. Maybe we should ice it."

"What for? It will fade away and hurt less and less. Believe me, I know," she said rather flippantly, but Buddy definitely didn't like it.

He pulled her to him lifted her up and placed her onto the counter. He pressed between her legs and held her face between his large, warm hands. "I don't want to hear such talk. You deserve to be pampered, cared for, and not to feel an ounce of pain or discomfort ever again." He kissed her deeply, and when he pulled back, she held on to his wrists.

"That's a beautiful consideration, Buddy, and oh how I wish that was even possible, but it's not realistic. Injuries happen. Bruises come and go."

"Not anymore. Not with us around to protect you and keep you safe and happy."

"Buddy, in your arms, being part of you now, that's what protects me and keeps me safe and warm. Just thinking about making love and feeling your lips against my skin can take away any remnants of bruises, pains, or fear. It's okay. This will heal."

"Okay, Nina. But just know that Trent, Johnny, and I will do whatever we can to keep you from feeling any pain again."

She smiled. "Thank you." She leaned forward and kissed him. As that kiss grew deeper, Buddy began to maneuver his hands under her tank and straight to her breasts. He was massaging them, pinching her nipples, and Nina was beginning to lose focus on what she needed to do. Like dropping off the pies to Sullivan's and meeting up with Cindy for some sort of outing. She had no idea, but with an extra fifty dollars to spend, she at least could feel a little normal and part of the crowd.

"Buddy," she whispered as he continued to lick and suckle her neck. He was pulling her tank top up over her head, and his eyes zeroed in on her breasts as he sucked in a breath.

"I love your body, Nina. Every fucking inch of it." He leaned forward and licked her cleavage then pressed the material on her breasts aside.

"Buddy, I need to deliver the pies."

"I'll get you there. But first, I'm going to have you here." He pulled her into his arms, walked toward the door, kicked it closed, and then carried her to her bedroom. As soon as he placed her feet back onto the rug, both of them began to divest one another of their clothing.

"We're going to be late."

"I don't give a fuck." He was naked and pushing her shorts down as she lost her balance and tumbled to the bed. She giggled as Buddy pulled off her shorts and tossed them behind him before spreading her thighs open with the palms of his hands.

"Take off that bra. I want to feast on you."

He leaned forward and licked up and down her pussy lips then plunged his tongue inside of her. She shook and squealed as she attempted to prop up on her elbows to remove her bra while Buddy feasted on her cream.

"Oh God," she said, out of breath as the clasp separated and she tossed her bra from her body. Buddy pulled her ass to the edge of the bed and aligned his cock with her cunt.

"I think making love to you is my new favorite thing to do on my lunch break." He shoved into her deeply. Nina moaned then grabbed his shoulders and pulled him down for a hug.

"Oh God, Buddy, you feel so big. This feels good. We're going to be very late."

"I'll make it worth your while. Hold on, honey." He began a series of deep, fast strokes as he lifted her thighs up and against his hips. She was resting on her shoulder blades, moaning from his every stroke.

"Never like this, Nina. Never."

He pumped his hips three more times, and she could feel his cock grow thicker. She was almost there herself, feeling tight, ready to explode. "Harder, Buddy. Harder," she ordered.

"Damn, baby." He moved so fast and so hard she screamed out his name as she orgasmed and fell to the bed. Buddy kept an arm wrapped around her waist as he continued to stroke into her at record speed. "So fucking good. You're mine, Nina. Mine." He exploded inside of her. They were both panting for breath as he pulled from her body, took her into his arms, and lay with her on her bed.

He leaned forward to kiss her then trailed his fingertip across her nipple and smiled. He squeezed her snugly. "Tonight, you sleep in our bed." He kissed her lips and then they heard his cell phone ringing.

"You'd better get that and I'd better go get washed up. After I drop off the pies, I'm going out with Cindy and some of her friends."

"Going out where?" he asked as he looked at his cell phone, standing there in all his naked gloriousness.

But she headed toward the bathroom to freshen up as he answered a call from work.

* * * *

Buddy was listening to Trent talking as he stepped back into his pants.

"Someone else saw our arsonist and described him exactly as Nina did."

"So that's good news, isn't it? Any leads on the guy?"

Buddy pulled on his shirt and began to button it up as Trent filled him in.

"The witness, she was assaulted last night. It's believed that the arsonist did it. He had to have found out about the reports."

"Oh shit. Nina?" Buddy said and turned around to the empty room. He knew she was in the bathroom freshening up. His chest tightened. He wouldn't take any chances.

"She's there with you now, right? You're dropping her off at Sullivan's to deliver the pies she made?"

"Yes, but then she made plans or something with Cindy and some friends."

"Shit, I don't know if this guy knows about Nina. Her name was never given or reported anywhere. You and I just headed to find her because we recognized her voice."

"Still, I'm not willing to take a chance. I just told her how I would protect her from harm and didn't even want her to feel the bruising she has from falling off that damn bike."

"She's bruised up from that?"

"Yes."

"Damn, are you sure it wasn't from us last night? I'd feel really bad if, you know, we got kind of wild with her."

"I asked her and she said no. She enjoyed last night as much as we did. Although, I would prefer if she moved in with us right now."

Just then Nina walked into the room, hands on her hips and shaking her head.

"Well, there goes surprising her and carrying her over the threshold tonight."

"She's there?"

"Just walked into the bedroom."

"The bedroom, huh? Aren't you on the clock, Detective?"

Buddy chuckled as Nina approached and he snagged her around the waist pulling her onto his thigh.

"She's my new favorite meal at lunch. You should try it."

Trent chuckled. "She'll be my dessert tonight."

"Who is that?" she whispered.

"Trent, he says you'll be his dessert tonight."

She crossed her arms in front of her chest. "That's pretty presumptuous of him."

"You heard her, right?"

"Tell her I said we'll discuss it later, and that it's nothing my thigh and my firm hand can't handle. Talk to you later." Buddy chuckled then repeated Trent's words.

"Does he mean he's going to spank me?" Her cheeks flushed. Buddy caressed her ass as she tried standing up only for him to pull her closer. He ran his hands under her shorts to her ass cheeks and squeezed.

"You have such a great ass, Nina. I'm certain my brothers and I will find any reason whatsoever to spank it, explore it, and of course fuck it." He pressed a finger to her puckered hole between her ass cheeks, and she pulled away, smacking his arm.

"Buddy!" she reprimanded and headed out of the room.

"Where are you going? I know you're all wet again."

"Stop that," she stated over her shoulder as he caught up to her, wrapped an arm around her waist from behind, and hugged her.

Buddy inhaled the scent of her shampoo and her skin. "You smell so good. I'm going to sleep like a baby with you in my arms tonight."

"We need to get going. The girls are going to be mad I'm late."

Buddy reached for the box of pies. "We need to talk about something on the way over."

"Is everything okay?" she asked, closing the door behind them and locking it.

"Just some precautions I want you to take."

"Okay," she said.

He couldn't help but to worry about Nina. She'd been through enough, now some stupid arsonist might find joy in harassing her? Great, just what they needed in Treasure Town. Again.

Chapter 8

Nina was laughing as Michaela told them a story about her boyfriends Jake McCurran and his brothers, Hal and Billy, who were firefighters.

"So just imagine Billy 'Bear' McCurran standing there staring at this horse that looked more like a large dog with a saddle on it." They were all laughing.

"The guy who owned the vineyard reprimanded the person who chose the horse for Bear. It was hysterical as Bear, who was trying to be a good sport, decided to climb onto the thing, and it sat down and then lay down completely. I nearly fell off my horse," Michaela told them, laughing even now.

"That is classic. How could anyone look at Bear, who is over six feet three, and even think he could sit on something so small?" Tasha asked.

"Well, come to find out hours later, after Bear got a new horse for the tour, that it was Jake and Hal who set the entire thing up."

"Oh my, I bet that caused a little bit of friction in the honeymoon suite," Serefina said.

"Well, actually it led to some very interesting foreplay and a bit of cowboy role-playing as well."

They hooted and hollered and Nina felt her cheeks blush as she giggled. "So you actually went to Tuscany? That is so amazing. I've never had the opportunity to travel," Nina told them.

"Well, neither did I until I headed to New York to see my sister, and then headed here."

"Can you tell her about that, Michaela? Nina is going through something pretty tough herself right now," Cindy said, and Nina wondered what was up. They had all spent the afternoon doing a little shopping and hooking Nina up with some thrift shops that had new, with-tag clothing for dirt cheap. At first she was embarrassed that everyone figured out she had four outfits to her name, but now things were different. Now she had at least six new ones.

"Of course I can. You see, Nina, I had a sister who I hadn't seen in many years because of the bad family life we had." As Michaela told her story, Nina sat there in awe of all she went through. Having some hit man after Michaela was similar to having Rico and his crew after Nina. Then when Tasha talked about working undercover for the feds and having to push the men she truly loved away from her as well as Serefina so they wouldn't get hurt or killed, Nina got the chills. She started thinking about the possibility that if Rico found her, she would do whatever it took to keep Trent, Buddy, and Johnny safe. Anything.

"Serefina had a serial arsonist after her. She nearly died in a fire, too," Tasha said, and then Serefina started adding her story.

Nina was enthralled with all the information. "I don't feel so out of sorts now and like some freak," Nina said as she finished telling them about Rico.

"Of course you aren't a freak. Men can be such assholes. It takes a lot to realize that they're messing with your head," Tasha told Nina.

"Yeah, and of course my boyfriends' cousins, Buddy, Trent, and Johnny, seem to be changing your opinion of men in general," Serefina teased and the others chuckled.

Nina looked down at her half-empty iced tea glass. "They're great men. Compassionate and caring, and I'm not used to that at all," she admitted.

Cindy placed her arm over her shoulder. "Don't worry, you'll get used to it. Something tells me those Landers men are never going to let you go. They adore you already."

Nina smiled and her cheeks warmed.

"We should have picked out some lingerie. A girl can never have enough sexy outfits to get her men wrapped around her finger," Tasha stated.

They giggled.

"So what are you going to do about the whole lack of ID, a cell phone, and business card thing?" Tasha asked.

"I don't know. I actually just got another order from one of the other restaurants near Angel's Wings. The owner saw my flier and then Fannie talked me up."

"That's great news. Before long you'll need your own bakery and some employees," Cindy stated.

"Let's not get too nuts. I think it will take a lot more time and definitely a lot more money."

"Well, if you need a backing, I can help you financially. Maybe even work it out so there's no real interest like a bank loan would have?" Michaela offered.

Nina was shocked but the others smiled. "I couldn't do that. You don't even know me, Michaela."

"Sure I do. Plus, us women need to stick together. Treasure Town is about making dreams come true, second chances, and opportunity to improve life and survive past indiscretions. Besides, I'm loaded. My sister somehow left me a lot of money. As you can tell by my stories, and from being in town for over a month, Jake is still the sheriff, and Billy and Hal are still firefighters. Everyone can do what it is that makes them happy. If need be, I could always help you with the books, organizing the business, or advertising, because that was what I used to do."

"Incredible," Nina said, feeling overwhelmed and so emotional about these people and their offers of help. A tear rolled down her cheek, and the women just stared at her, smiling. "I never even had a friend before, and you're offering me—a perfect stranger—so much help. I can't get over it."

"You have more than a friend, Nina. You have four friends right here," Cindy said and they all agreed.

Serefina brought up another topic and the conversation continued around Nina. She felt her spirits lift and her enthusiasm rise just thinking about the possibilities and potential opportunities she had here in Treasure Town. Maybe even three men she could spend the rest of her life with and love forever.

* * * *

Johnny was waiting for Nina as she pulled up in the SUV with Tasha and the girls. They said hello, dropped her off, and then Nina came out carrying a bag with her.

"Hey, baby, I missed you." Johnny pulled her into his arms and kissed her. The women honked the horn and whistled and hollered out the window and Johnny chuckled as he shook his head.

Johnny followed Nina up the stairs to her apartment. "You had a good time I gather?"

"Oh yes, it was a lot of fun. Those women are so kind and very easy to talk to," she said, tossing her bag onto the couch.

"What's in the bag?"

"Just some clothes. I guess the fact that I only own four outfits stands out."

"You look sexy in anything, although I love you in nothing at all." He pulled her closer and began kissing her again. Nina wrapped her arms around his shoulders and kissed Johnny back. He lifted her up and she straddled his waist as he carried her over to the couch.

He placed her down next to it and began to lift her tank top.

"Buddy was concerned about the bruising on your hip."

"Buddy was?" she whispered, sounding breathless.

He stared at her lips, moved closer, and kissed her quickly, pulling her lower lip between his teeth and giving it a tug. "I should really be sure that you're okay."

He turned her around and pressed her body over the arm of the sofa so that she was leaning on her forearms.

"I love your body, Nina. I thought of it all day at work."

She looked over her shoulder at him in such a sexy seductive way. He licked his lips and she lifted her ass toward him. It seemed his Nina was just as aroused as he was.

Using his palms, Johnny smoothed them along her back, her waist, and over her short shorts, giving her ass a squeeze.

He slowly pulled them down, and the little vixen lifted her thighs and maneuvered out of them. Now she was naked, only wearing that black sexy bra that barely covered her breasts. He leaned over her and gave his hips a pump against her ass. She moaned.

Caressing along her hips, he slid his hands underneath her as he knelt on the couch behind her. "Fuck, these tits are big, baby."

She shivered and smiled as he leaned lower to kiss her skin. The feel of her warm flesh against his lips brought on a surge of possessiveness.

"Did you miss me, Nina?"

"Yes," she replied quickly. He smoothed his hands back to her hips and leaned down to explore the bruising from her fall. He pressed his lips over each marking and then trailed a finger down the crack of her ass, over her puckered hole, and straight to her wet cunt. He thrust a finger up into her and Nina moaned aloud.

"Oh God, Johnny, I can't take it. Please do something."

She pushed her ass back against him, and he moved a hand over her hip to hold her there while he finger-fucked her.

"I am doing something. I'm getting this wet, tight pussy ready for cock." He pulled his finger out as she pushed her ass back at him. "Unless you want my cock someplace else, Nina?" He pressed his finger to her puckered hole and slipped it inside.

"Oh. My. God." She moaned.

"Fuck, Nina, you make me crazy."

He gently pulled his finger from her ass and tore off his clothing. He was back behind her adjusting his position over her as she gripped the arm of the coach, pushed her ass back toward him, and began to slowly rock up and down. He moved over her body, caressing a palm over her thigh to her belly and pressed two digits up into her cunt.

"Oh, Johnny, please," she blurted out with her chin tilted forward.

He moved against her, his cock hitting her pussy and his fingers.

"Tell me where you want me, baby."

"Everywhere," she blurted out.

He pulled his fingers from her cunt and moved them in front of her to her lips. "Suck them, Nina. Taste how fucking sweet you are." She did, and when he felt her tongue twirl over and between his cream-covered fingers, he used his other hand to adjust his cock and thrust into her from behind.

"Yes. Oh God, yes, more."

"Fuck, Nina, you're wild. I love it." He grabbed her hips and began a series of long, deep thrusts into her pussy. Nina kept pushing back, counterthrusting and trying to give him more pleasure. He licked along her shoulder as he stroked deeper, faster into her. The couch squeaked and the sound of her dripping cream, his balls slapping her ass, drove him further over the edge. He felt Nina tighten up, and before she came, before he lost himself within her, he pulled out.

"Oh!" She hung her head.

"You said everywhere, baby, didn't you?" he whispered as he stroked his fingers into her cunt and then over her puckered hole. She thrust back and forth against his fingers.

"That's right, Nina, you get that ass ready for cock, 'cause I'm going to give it to you good."

He licked down her spine then between her ass cheeks, stroking her anus. Back and forth he slid his tongue, wetting her, lubricating her as he thrust two fingers up into her pussy.

"Oh God, Johnny, just do it already please." He squeezed her ass and she gasped.

"Demanding little thing, aren't you? Okay, baby, here I come." He slowly began to press his cock against her puckered hole. He leaned back and watched the mushroom top begin to breach her ass, and his heart rate increased, his brow filled with perspiration, and the need to fuck and claim her filled his soul.

She pressed back and he pushed forward at the same time, sinking his cock into her ass. He squeezed her cheeks and she moaned louder and rocked back and forth.

"Here we go, baby. Here we go." He leaned over her again, ran his hands down her arms to her hands, which she had braced on the arm of the couch. He started to rock into her, moving and thrusting his hips, filling her ass with cock. She moaned with every stroke and then she lifted a hand and moved it to her pussy.

"Are you touching yourself, Nina?"

"Yes," she hissed.

"You're a god damn fantasy, baby. I love that you're so aroused and touching yourself."

"You do it to me Johnny," she told him, and he felt wild and as if he were on a high.

"You drive me wild. I want to get lost inside of you, Nina. Inside of you is heaven." He kissed her neck and suckled along the skin as he pumped his hips faster. She spread her thighs wider, fingered herself and moaned as she stretched further over the arm of the couch. His cock felt so damn hard as he shoved deeper into her ass while she moaned and pushed back.

"I've got you, baby. I've got you." He began a rapid pace, gripped her hips, and pounded into her ass then held her hip with one hand as he maneuvered his other hand over her waist, down her belly, then over her fingers that were thrusting into her pussy. He moved his fingers over hers. She moaned when he massaged her clit and rubbed circles with her cream before shoving his fingers into her cunt. When he did, he thrust his cock into her ass and his fingers into her wet cunt. Nina screamed her release. It was all too much, too erotic to handle, and he pumped his hips then thrust hard and fast until he finally lost it holding her tight, his body flush against hers and released his seed.

He moved his fingers, cupped her breasts, then glided his palms along her hips and ass massaging her muscles.

"You're perfect for me, Nina. Abso-fucking-lutely perfect." She chuckled and he slowly pulled from her ass, turned her around, and hugged her to him. They didn't bother with their clothing as they cuddled up on the couch until she fell asleep in his arms.

* * * *

Buddy and Trent along with Jake stood watching the blaze. The sirens blared as more units arrived to assist Ladder 19 put out the fire. Across town in the industrial park where many businesses had their storage facilities, one very large building was burning to the ground. The firefighters worked to control the blaze and to prevent the fire from spreading to the adjacent buildings surrounding them.

"Who owns that building?" Buddy asked Jake.

"I don't know. Why?"

"Well, we need to find out. Trent and I are coming up with some odd connections to the places that have been hit by this arsonist. Take into account Nina's description of the guy, what he was wearing, and then the descriptions we received after interviewing some of the other witnesses, and there are some connections."

"Like what? You think you may know who this guy is?" Jake asked.

"Not specifically who he is, but perhaps what his agenda might be. We can't be certain. For example, the guy is always wearing a red jersey. Nina said she thought it had a weird word like Costa on it. We're thinking Coastal Bay, a few towns over."

"Shit. Well maybe the guy's from there?" Jake asked.

"We're running a few scenarios. Maybe you could see if there have been any people arrested for arson crimes in Coastal Bay over the last year or so. Nina as well as the other witnesses from the last fire thought that it was a teenager. It very well could be and that's why the extent of damage has been minimal," Buddy stated.

"But he did assault one witness, who now is afraid to stay involved with the investigation," Trent added.

"You seriously think some teenager is responsible for all of this and even the assault?" Jake asked, appearing annoyed.

"We've had our share of delinquent teens setting shit on fire for fun and attention," Buddy added.

"We've also got some serious competition between the schools along the shorelines. Baseball, especially," Trent said.

Buddy widened his eyes. "You think this about a sports rivalry?"

"Shit, that could very well be. A few years back, well, more than that actually—I wasn't even the sheriff yet—there was some major brawling going on between the high schools. The police had to respond to a lot of fights between the athletes."

"Anything more recently, Jake?" Buddy asked.

"I don't think so. Not since the boards got together and decided to contact the owner of the property bordering Treasure Town and Fairway and come up with developing one major sports facility. The reaction has been positive."

"Maybe this individual just wants to cause trouble and get things brewing," Trent suggested.

"He could have killed someone. Then add in the fact that he assaulted the woman who was a witness," Buddy added.

"Well, the other witnesses have been notified of the assault. They all go to the high school. Then of course there's Nina. But we put her name into the system as Valez, just as precaution because of the other situation," Jake informed them.

"We appreciate that. Any news from Rye's friend in the government?" Trent asked Jake.

"Not yet. But I hear that Nina's pie-baking business is really doing well. Michaela offered to help her set up shop in town."

"Really? Nina didn't mention that," Trent said.

"Michaela did mention that Nina was a bit taken aback by the offer. But you know Michaela, she has a big heart, she knows a lot about business and advertising. She would be a huge help to Nina. Then add in all the people she knows, and she could just about help Nina with every aspect of the business. I think even Cindy is interested in helping Nina, too."

"That is amazing. I guess we'll talk to Nina about it tonight. Maybe we can ease her mind about the offer. She's so afraid to accept help from anyone. It's like she feels she'll owe them her soul."

"That's understandable, considering what you said this ex of hers did to her," Jake replied.

"Hey, I was just thinking. Is there a common connection between the places this guy has set fire to and the witnesses at the school? Are they all connected to Treasure Town or Coastal Bay somehow?" Buddy asked, interrupting the current topic.

"Well, the witnesses are all students at the high school here in Treasure Town. Um…the owner of the liquor store has a son that goes to school there," Jake offered.

"Any chance he plays baseball?" Buddy asked.

Jake widened his eyes. "I think he does. But why would baseball be the target and not any other sports or even all of them?" Jake asked.

"Nina said the arsonist was wearing a Yankees baseball cap. Just throwing some ideas around here. I think we need to find out who owns this particular storage facility and also the connection to the other small fires. Maybe question them and see if any threats had been made to them prior to the fires. Perhaps even minor things that were sort of suspicious."

"That's a good idea, Buddy. Let's see what we can come up with," Trent said.

"I'll take care of things on my end. Oh, are you guys going to the Station Friday night? My dad and Jerome have the stage all set up and running now. There'll be local bands playing there every Friday and Saturday night."

"Awesome. Yeah, we'll be there," Buddy told him. Then Jake headed over to the fire truck to talk to the fire chief.

"Hey, that was really nice of Michaela to offer to help Nina. Do you think she'll accept the help?"

"No. I think she'll fight it every step of the way."

"Maybe we can talk her into it. It's not like it would be any easier if we offered to help."

"I wish she would let us. I mean, we've made major progress and all, but I can't help but to worry about her. I know her scars run deep. Allowing us to make love to her was a huge step. I'm afraid if we push for more too soon she'll panic."

"I get that feeling, too, Trent, but that doesn't mean I'm going to hold back my feelings. The time we spent today was incredible. The only reason why I don't feel nervous, worried, and sick to my stomach right now is because I know that Johnny is with her. She's learning about all of us individually. That's what we wanted."

"You're right. But I have to say, taking her together was fucking incredible."

Buddy smiled. "She's incredible. Let's do what we can tonight and then head home. I can call Johnny and see if he made dinner or if we should pick something up."

"Sounds good. I'll just check a few things out with the chief."

Buddy called Johnny's cell, and when he didn't answer he couldn't help but to wonder if he was in bed with Nina after making love to her today, too.

He smiled as he walked over toward Trent and the fire chief to get more information.

* * * *

Johnny stared at Nina's back and ass as she continued sleeping. He had reached over to grab his phone and texted Buddy back and Nina didn't even move. The poor woman was exhausted. She was working so hard, baking twenty pies every couple of days, and the orders were doubling. He had smiled when he heard Mercury and Jenks, two other paramedics, talk about these new homemade delicious pies being served at Sullivan's. Those were Nina's pies. His Nina.

He smiled then trailed his finger along the curve of her hips and ass. She had a fantastic ass. He'd never felt so possessive before. He looked back down at the light-red lines along her lower back and ass. They were faint but noticeable when she was like this, naked and spread out on the couch next to him. His cock instantly hardened and he would love to make love to her again. Maybe with Buddy and Trent coming home and meeting them here at her apartment, it would mean the three of them taking her together again. That had been life altering.

She was truly a part of each of them now, and he would never let her go. He wanted to make her happy, make her smile and feel the love she deserved to feel.

In the distance he heard the truck pull up in the driveway then the doors close. Johnny was glad he'd texted Buddy telling him to use his key. Nina stirred slightly and he watched her lift her ass and then get comfortable again, pressing her ass toward his hip. His cock twitched, hitting her thigh. He smiled and then ran the palm of his hand along her back.

"What time is it?" she asked, sounding all groggy and sexy.

"Dinnertime." He trailed a finger down the crack of her ass. He pressed lower and she moaned but also parted her thighs. His woman loved to be touched by him.

He pressed lower until his fingers made contact with her pussy, swollen, wet, ready for exploration. He thrust a finger up into her then heard her moan. The door to the apartment opened and Nina jerked her head up. Johnny held her in place.

He smiled as he locked gazes with Trent and Buddy, who immediately took in the sight of Nina, naked and aroused on the couch. He wondered if they could see his finger between her thighs.

"What do we have here?" Trent asked as he passed the pizza boxes to Buddy, who smiled and took them.

"Just waking Sleeping Beauty for dinner. She's very wet, though."

Trent rubbed his hands together as he approached and then squatted down next to the couch. Johnny continued to thrust his fingers up into her as Trent cupped her face and held her gaze.

"You look well loved and well rested."

He leaned forward and kissed her. Nina began to turn her hip, and Johnny maneuvered in front of her, lifting her thigh and spreading her wide as she rolled to her back.

"I think desert is in order first," Buddy said from behind Trent as he started undressing.

* * * *

Trent absorbed the feel of Nina's body and the way she responded to Johnny arousing her. His own cock hardened and he wanted nothing more than to sink balls-deep into her cunt and love her.

"Are you hungry?" Trent asked her.

She reached up and cupped his chin then caressed his whiskers. "For you."

He felt the instant need and hunger for her as he cupped her breast and leaned down to lick and suckle her nipple. "I'm hungry for you, too. Every inch of you, baby."

"I want you now. All three of you." Her cheeks turned a nice shade of red. She was so sweet. His heart soared.

Trent stood up, tossing off his shirt. Johnny climbed over the couch, and Buddy sat down, taking Nina into his arms to straddle his waist.

He kissed her deeply as Trent moved in behind her, caressing her ass.

"I missed you," Buddy told her.

"I missed you, too." She cupped his cheeks and kissed him as Buddy aligned his cock with her pussy and she slid down, taking him in. The sight aroused Trent even more as he held his cock in his hand and stroked the long, thick muscle. With a hand on her hip he bent down and began to lick and nibble Nina's ass. She moaned and Johnny was there moving something behind the couch.

"What are you doing?" she asked, sounding breathless as she thrust up and down on Buddy. Trent looked up and saw Johnny lifting a small stool. He stood on it behind the couch and now his cock was up higher. Nina chuckled.

"Hey, I want to feel that hot, sexy mouth while my brothers fuck you, but I didn't think Buddy would appreciate my cock next to his cheek."

"Fuck no," Buddy said then pulled Nina's breast into his mouth and suckled it.

Trent laughed, blowing warm breath against Nina's puckered hole. He spread her ass cheeks and licked along the bud. "Are you ready for me, Nina?" Trent asked then licked up and down the crack over her anus. He pressed a finger to it and pushed in.

"Oh God, yes. Yes."

"Come here," Johnny whispered.

Trent looked over Nina's shoulder and watched her take Johnny's cock into her mouth. He thrust his finger into her ass as Buddy's hands squeezed onto her hip bones and lifted her up and down. Trent could hear Buddy suckling Nina's breast, holding on to it and tugging. He could only picture it since his view was obstructed by Nina's back and glorious ass.

"Fuck, baby, you got me," Trent whispered. He pulled out his finger and replaced it with his cock, pressing into her anus.

Nina moaned and Johnny grunted as he rocked against the couch. Buddy stilled for a moment while Trent worked his cock into her ass. He pulled slightly out then pushed deeper and deeper until he was fully seated in her ass.

"Grrr." He growled and leaned over her, his thighs pressed against the back of her thighs.

It was so amazing, the feeling of completion, a connection like he'd never felt. Making love to Nina with his brothers strengthened their bond, their brotherhood, like never before. He felt so hard, so aroused that he knew he wouldn't last long. It was such an out-of-control feeling that he knew was a losing battle. They worked in sync, stroking, thrusting, sucking. The sounds and grunts that echoed in the room were so wild and erotic that he grew thicker.

"Oh, baby, I'm coming, Nina. This mouth is too much. This fucking body is too much," Johnny said. Trent thrust harder, faster, and held on to Nina's shoulders, pulling her slightly back. It gave him a view of her mouth sucking Johnny's cock in and out and Buddy's mouth sucking her nipple as Johnny held it out to his brother like an offering of a feast.

"Fuck that's hot. Holy shit, I love it," Trent told them, and Johnny grunted, released her breast, grabbed Nina's hair, and moaned as he shot his seed down her throat. She was slurping, licking, and suckling his cum until Johnny cursed and jumped back.

It was Buddy and Trent now, and Trent knew he wouldn't last much longer.

"I'm there, baby. I'm right fucking there."

The sounds of his thighs slapping against her thighs was so wild he lost control. Trent grunted and held himself deep in her ass, making her scream her release as he shot his seed. He thrust two more times then felt Buddy lifting Nina up and down on his shaft. Trent pulled from her ass, making her moan and then fall forward against

Buddy's chest. He was pumping his hips upward at record speed. Nina was moaning and then sat up and counterthrust on top of him.

It was a sight to see, Nina's tits bouncing, Buddy's face bright red, the veins by his temples pulsating, and then they both moaned and came together. Buddy wrapped his arms around her so tight she was lost in his embrace.

"I love you, Nina. I fucking love you," Buddy told her and Trent felt his heart tighten. This was serious. An intense moment. Nina pulled back and stared at Buddy, breathing rapidly and holding his gaze.

Buddy cupped her breasts and ran his thumbs along the nipples.

"You don't have to say anything. When the time is right, when you feel it and know it's true and you mean it, say it then."

She wrapped her arms around his neck and squeezed him tight as tears fell from her eyes. Trent smiled at Buddy and Johnny.

They were all in love with her already. Nina was going to be theirs forever.

Chapter 9

Rico stood by the bar on the top floor of the club. It was a private area he used for business meetings and entertaining important clients. As the music blared and people drank, danced, and enjoyed the nightlife, he stood there anticipating the meeting with trepidation and anger.

Miguel and Martino had expressed their upset over Nina's disappearance. Martino found out what actually happened to get Nina to leave, and now he was taking over and minimizing Rico's role in the club business. It didn't help matters to find out that the feds were investigating Rico on over a dozen accusations of murder, attempted murder, grand larceny, illegal gambling, and a list of other shit that would put him behind bars for life.

Rico lifted the shot glass to his lips and drank the contents. He would need more than a buzz to get through this meeting with Martino and Miguel. He would need a goddamn miracle and for Nina to be found. He was paying those investigators good money to track her. Where the fuck did she go? How was she making money? The thought of her prostituting flashed through his mind.

Not my Nina.

Part of her appeal to Miguel and Martino was her virginity. They knew he'd had her first and took that, but even when they eventually would take her together, he had insisted that he be her first. She had become a bonus to the deal they were going into together that included a new line of clubs in Puerto Rico.

He knew he was going to have to do some smooth talking. Hell, he might have to still allow Miguel and Martino to share Nina with him to save face. It would suck, but who the fuck knew where the bitch had hidden out all these months and who she'd fucked. The thought enraged him even more.

She had become an asset and maybe even a liability. It all depended on where she was, who she had been with, and what trouble it could cause for Rico. She was very appealing, to the point of being unable to blend in. Her eyes alone were mesmerizing. It was ironic that once again Nina would be a grand prize to a sweet deal.

The door to the room opened and Cougar was there.

"Boss, their car pulled up outside."

"Start the music, get the women ready, and bring them up, Cougar. Remember, we need to appease their every demand or it could fuck up a multimillion-dollar deal."

"You got it. Good luck."

I'm going to need a hell of a lot more than that. I'm going to need Nina.

* * * *

Nina didn't know what was going on, but Cindy had blindfolded her and then helped her get into Michaela's SUV. Tasha, Serefina, Florence, Cindy, Tasha's cousin Melanie, and their friends Catalina and Mel were all in the SUV. They were giggling and talking about going to the Station tomorrow night and about some guy band. Mel was describing one of the members, a firefighter and a guitarist.

"He is gorgeous and has a kick-ass body. He plays the guitar like a pro and, most importantly, he is single."

They laughed and cheered, encouraging Mel to make a move Friday night, and Nina just sat there feeling foolish with her blindfold.

"How come I'm the only one wearing a blindfold?" she asked.

"Because this is your surprise," Serefina said and then the SUV slowed down. Nina realized that they weren't very far from the boardwalk, and if she weren't mistaken, they were in the business district that had small shops and little places to eat, have drinks, buy specialty gifts and things. She liked it down here, and it was not as noisy and crowded as the boardwalk a couple of blocks up.

Michaela parked the truck and Nina could hear the women getting all excited as they climbed out and then Nina's door opened. Cindy helped her out, then walked a few steps.

"Okay. Now, we're going to take off the blindfold and I want you to not focus instantly on first impressions but more so on potential."

She didn't know what that meant, but then the blindfold was undone. As her eyes adjusted to the sunlight, she saw the small old-fashioned house. It looked like it was about to fall down. Around it were nicer stores, but this one was bigger and needed a lot of work.

She looked at all their expectant faces, not quite understanding what was happening.

"She doesn't get it," Florence said.

"She hasn't a clue," Tasha added, crossing her arms and smiling.

"What is it? What am I supposed to see?" Nina asked.

"You're supposed to see the potential. This is going to be Nina's Homemade Pies and Bakery, or whatever you want to call it. I bought it cheap, and we're going to fix it up and get you your own store right here in the center of the busiest businesses in town," Michaela stated.

Nina felt a lump form in her throat. She had a million questions flying through her head. How was she going to pay for this? What money would she use to fix this up? She couldn't do something like this alone with no help.

"I think she's going to pass out," Melanie said. Michaela grabbed her and held her by her side.

"Nina, you're not alone in this. Trust me. Trust us, your friends, to help you. We've been working it all out and trying to come up with a way to help you establish your business and make your dreams come true."

"Yes, we're all chipping in. Cindy and Melanie need jobs and they know how to bake and cook. Florence offered her assistance when needed, and Mel, well, she's great at customer service and greeting people," Michaela told her.

"I'm able to redo this whole place," Michaela told her. "I mean renovate it so it looks welcoming, comfortable, and appealing to the eye. It will stand out more than any other place, and we can put in industrial ovens, all the things you need as a professional baker. I got the place cheap because it really does need a lot of work."

"Oh, my neighbor Ike Mason is also looking for side work, so he can be our delivery guy. Between all the people we know in Treasure Town, we'll have this place up and running in months. You'll be right there helping along the way and designing things like you dreamed of," Michaela added.

Nina felt the tears fill her eyes and then she lost it.

"I don't know what to say. No one has ever done anything so amazing for me before. I'll never be able to pay you all back," she said.

Cindy pulled her into a hug as a couple of cars pulled up behind Michaela's SUV. "Sure you will, by being our friend and knowing we're always here for you, and you can always be here for all of us."

"How did she take it?" Jake asked as he, Buddy, Trent, and Johnny arrived, smiling. The other vehicle had two men in it Nina didn't know.

"Meet Billy and Hal, Jake's brothers and my men," Michaela said with a wink as the big guy, Billy, pulled her into a hug and smiled at Nina.

"Welcome to Treasure Town, doll," he said.

Nina felt Trent's arms move around her waist as he hugged her from behind.

"You've made quite the impression on everyone, Nina. Accept all our help and let us make your dreams come true."

She smiled wide as the tears still flowed. "Thank you. I'll never forget this day, this moment, and what you've all done."

"We need to get back to work. How about we celebrate at the Station tomorrow night?" Jake suggested. They all cheered.

Nina stood there a moment and stared at the building.

Her very own storefront. She could practically see it now. The large front porch where people could sit and enjoy the goodies she made and even a gourmet coffee from the coffee bar. There would be seats inside, all the pies on display, and a kitchen where she could make at least a dozen pies at a time. She smiled at she looked at Cindy and pulled her next to her. "You'll really help me? I mean work with me here?"

"If you'll hire me, boss," she teased.

"Thank you so much, Cindy. Thank you." She hugged Cindy and then the girls started talking about all the different possibilities until Trent, Johnny, and Buddy pulled her between them and took turns kissing her.

"We'll see you later tonight?"

"You betcha," she said and watched them leave.

She looked around the streets at all the little places so perfectly done up and brand new. Her place was going to look beautiful when they were finished. This was going to be the beginning of a new life, a fresh start, and her future here in Treasure Town.

* * * *

Rye Hawkins sat in Jake's office waiting for Buddy and Trent to arrive. Jake didn't like what Rye had told him so far about the men working for Rico who might be looking for her.

"So they're pretty serious about this woman?" Rye asked Jake.

"I'd say so. I'm happy for them. The three of them deserve to finally meet someone special and settle down."

"Yeah, I hear she's easy on the eyes and bakes a mean apple pie."

Jake chuckled.

Just then Buddy and Trent arrived, entered Jake's office, then shook hands with Rye. Jake walked over and closed the door.

He then leaned against his desk and crossed his arms in front of his chest. "Okay, Rye, tell us what you found out," Jake said.

Rye took a deep breath and began. "Well, as you know, the state police are initially the ones who investigate illegal gambling across the state and its borders. This guy Rico, who is currently out in California, gained the attention of not only the state police and their investigation into illegal gambling, but also the feds. Looks like more recently he started joining forces, doing business with two men who are high-profile smugglers."

"High-profile smugglers?" Jake asked.

"Amongst other things. From what my buddy explained to me, these two men are being monitored and have been for quite some time by both the state police and the federal government. They have been really pushing this construction agenda in Puerto Rico and the feds believe it to be a front for more illegal gambling. Through their initial investigation, wire taps, surveillance, and inside agents, they know these two men and Rico are partnering up."

"Wow, does this mean that the feds and the state police are preparing to bust them soon?" Buddy asked.

"They're looking for a big hit. They don't want the petty stuff, but actual big shipments of drugs, all their locations where gambling occur, and whatever else they can pull together in one nice neat bow. Problem is, as many undercover guys the feds and state police have in there, there are more working in the departments blowing the whistle before the cops can get close and take them out. Rico is really more of a loan shark, a guy who flips the bill and gets paid double. He works it out and has his crew of shit that rough up the nonpaying gamblers. You know the deal. You've had to deal with this shit around here for years."

"That we have. It's a vicious cycle. As soon as we think we've cleared out the trash, we wind up finding more popping up around the county," Jake said.

"These men, the ones who work for Rico and do his dirty work, are they the ones who he would send to look for her?" Trent asked. Buddy crossed his arms in front of his chest and stood there in a protective stance.

"That's the thing. My guy is trying to find out if your woman's name has even been tossed around among the feds or troopers as someone to speak to. You know, like an informant or witness to Rico's crimes."

"God, I didn't even think of that. Nina said that he never spoke about his businesses," Buddy added.

"Well, no need to worry about that right now, he hasn't heard a thing about her. Hopefully the federal and state investigation will erupt and this guy Rico will go to jail for life. Then Nina won't have to worry ever again," Rye said.

"But if he doesn't, and they don't move on this, she'll always worry and so will we," Trent replied.

They were quiet for a few seconds and then Jake changed the subject. "I got the damn media all over my ass now about this arsonist. Someone leaked the info that it may be a teenager."

"Shit, the kid already attacked one witness, if he thinks someone else ratted him out or could identify him, he may become violent again," Trent said.

"I think we need to look at some of these kids from all the local high schools. I've got a list of twelve who were brought in by some law enforcement agency or reported by their school principals for starting fires or burning things. It's a better start than any," Buddy said.

"We could split them up and each go question these kids," Trent suggested.

"Sounds good to me," Jake said.

Buddy turned toward Rye. "We appreciate everything you're doing to help us protect Nina. She's terrified by this man. So if you hear about his arrest or anything, please let us know."

"You got it. I'll keep you posted," Rye said. Then he stood up and shook Jake's hand before heading out of the room.

"She'll be okay, guys. We're going to stay on top of this and not let our guard down," Jake told them.

"We're definitely not taking any chances," Trent said before he looked at Jake, then his brother, and walked out of the office.

"I don't think I've ever seen Trent like this," Jake told Buddy as they walked to the door.

"That's because he's never been in love before. You know the deal. Now he just needs to admit it and tell Nina."

Jake's eyes widened and an "oh" left his lips. "Yeah, I can see that being a tough one for him. But honesty is the best policy. Eventually he'll come clean and tell her."

Buddy chuckled. "Is that how it was with Michaela?"

"Hell, Michaela was and still is a piece of work. When she gets something in her mind, there's no stopping her."

"What she's doing for Nina is really awesome. She never would have accepted anything like that from Trent, Johnny, and me."

"No, she wouldn't have. But could you blame her, Buddy? I mean this guy really did a fucking number on her. It's surprising she even let you guys this close."

Buddy released a sigh as he looked out the door toward the main office in the sheriff's department and spotted Trent talking with Rye Hawkins and Rye's brother, Deputy Turbo Hawkins.

"I think Trent and her have a lot of the same fears when it comes to trust and showing scars. That common ground brought us all together."

"I believe it. She's got a new home here, and already a bunch of new friends. We'll do whatever needs to be done to keep her safe."

"I appreciate that, Jake. We'll see you tonight at the Station?"

"I'll be there," Jake said, and Buddy smiled, looking forward to bringing Nina to the Station and showing her off as their woman.

* * * *

Nina stared at herself in the mirror. Who would have thought that a thrift store could have such beautiful clothing? The pale-pink dress hugged her hips and accentuated her large breasts. She hoped that Buddy, Johnny, and Trent liked it and didn't think it was too sexy. The pale-pink color was sweet and pretty, and it was a designer dress, tags and all, for $10.00.

She slipped into the high-heel sandals, also from the thrift shop, hardly used and a perfect fit. She brushed her long brown locks into a makeshift pony on the side of her head and let it flow over her shoulder. Her hair partially covered her cleavage.

She stared at her bare neck and wished for a moment she had something to wear. Some kind of locket or jewelry that belonged only to her. But those thoughts had been long gone for months. She wondered why she even cared about something like that now.

"Nina, we're going to be late. Just put something casual on. You'll look beautiful in anything," Johnny yelled from the living room. She chuckled. That was Johnny, her sweet, compassionate paramedic. He was always so thoughtful and caring. She bet his patients, the people he needed to help and sometimes even save, adored him instantly.

She took a deep breath and grabbed the small purse, also from the thrift shop. Her lips looked pretty with the soft pink lip gloss Serefina insisted she grab, but nothing else. No makeup. She didn't really even like the stuff.

She took a deep breath and walked out of her bedroom.

Johnny whistled. Buddy stood up from the couch, appearing shocked. And Trent? Well, Trent looked angry. She pulled her lip between her teeth then stopped herself because of the lip gloss she wore.

"Okay, let's go," she said, trying to avoid their criticism, disapproval, or dislike of the outfit. Whatever reason they stared at her for, it made her want to run for the door. Before she made it there, Johnny snagged her around the waist and pulled her close. "Damn, baby, you look so gorgeous. Wow." He kissed her neck.

Buddy walked closer and stared down into her eyes. "Where did you get this?"

"A place the girls and I went shopping last week." She still wondered what he was thinking and then he reached out to trail a finger down the bodice.

"It's kind of low cut, isn't it?" he asked. She looked down and shook her head just as he cupped her breast, reached for her cheek, and held her face.

"You're one sexy lady, Nina. I love this on you, and I'm going to be keeping you real close." He leaned forward and kissed her. She closed her eyes, was lost in his gentle kiss and his possessive words, which warmed her body through.

"Let me take a look," Trent interrupted.

Buddy released her lips and stepped to the side. There stood Trent, hands on his hips as he evaluated her attire. God, the man was so fucking gorgeous. His brown eyes bore into hers, and she swallowed hard. She would never want to be on their wrong side. They were that intimidating.

He reached down to take her hand and slowly brought it up to his lips. He kissed the top of it and smiled.

"You need to dress like this for us more often, doll. You're stunning."

"Thank you. I guess we should go, huh?" she asked, feeling nervous and very horny. She would love to skip this night and get right to bed with her three men. The thought of calling them that aroused her even more.

"I don't know what you're thinking right now, but if it's what I'm thinking, which is stay here and have my way with your body, I'm in," Trent said.

"We can't do that. We promised we would show up. Everyone is going to be there and I can't wait to finally see this place everyone raves about," Nina told him.

"Well, then let's go, but we're not staying late. I want to get back here so we can explore what's hiding underneath that dress," Johnny said. Nina walked ahead of him between Buddy and Trent, who chuckled.

"Oh, that's easy. Nothing." She sashayed out the door and down the steps. He stopped her by the truck, pulled her into his arms, and held her firmly with his eyebrows scrunched up.

"Did you say that you're not wearing any undergarments?" Johnny asked.

Trent and Buddy watched and waited.

"Maybe I am, maybe I'm not." Before Johnny could reach under her dress to check, she swatted his hand and got into the truck right in the front between Trent and Buddy.

"You are very naughty, Nina. You know what I do when my woman's naughty?" Johnny asked, leaning forward from the backseat. She tilted her head back, exposing her breasts to his view. He inched his fingers over her shoulder straight to her cleavage. He stuck his hand inside and his eyes widened. Now he knew she wore no bra.

"A spanking. You're going to get a spanking. And if you aren't wearing any panties, I may just have a little taste of you right back here in the truck on the way home." He squeezed her breast again and she nearly moaned.

"We'll see, Johnny. That all depends on whether or not you behave."

She turned around, causing him to remove his hand and sit back as Trent drove the truck out of the driveway.

"Sounds like a challenge to me, bro," Buddy said.

Johnny rubbed his hands together and smiled. "I love me a challenge, especially when the prize is my sweet, horny little Nina."

"Johnny!" she reprimanded, but Trent and Buddy chuckled. She sat there trying to calm her body and the desire to jump over the seat and give Johnny the ride of his life.

She'd come a long way in a short period of time with these men. Every day she was falling deeper and deeper in love with them. She wondered why she still held back from telling them that she loved them.

Because I'm still scared of getting hurt and being used. When will these feelings disappear?

* * * *

Nina was really enjoying the Station. It was such a cool place with lots of memorabilia and old pictures everywhere. She could spend hours looking at them. The band was playing, their first performance at the Station. Hal, Billy, Jake's dad, Burt, and his friend Jerome had installed a new stage. It was going to be a regular Friday and Saturday night event with bands and talent performing for the patrons.

Johnny wrapped his arms around her waist and pulled her close. She felt his lips against her neck and his hand squeezed her hip bone. She noticed that Trent, Buddy, and especially Johnny were really being affectionate. Their public display was obviously done to warn off any other men. Truth was, she didn't mind at all. She felt so comfortable with them. She really hoped that this relationship worked out, because the thought of losing them or something going wrong to break them apart instantly made her feel sick. She had this burning tightness in her chest. It scared her and she turned in Johnny's arms and hugged him tight.

His hands caressed her back. One slid over her ass and squeezed it quickly before turning to her back.

"Are you okay?" he whispered.

God, he's so amazing and in tune to me.

She wanted to tell him that she loved him and that she never wanted to be apart but feared he would find her clingy. Which was exactly what she was doing right now, clinging to his neck, trying to pull his scent, his cologne, all Johnny into her and ease this uncertainty and fear she was suddenly overwhelmed with. Nina needed to pull it together.

She swallowed hard.

"I just like hugging you. It feels good in your arms, Johnny."

His concerned expression turned into a smile. His lip curled. He got that sexy, flirty twinkle in his eye, and he licked his lower lip. "You feel good in my arms, too, baby. Better than anything."

She kissed him softly on the lips, and he pulled her tighter and explored her mouth deeply, making her moan. She had to get it together, so she pressed against his chest and eased her lips from his. She stepped back, needing a reprieve before their make-out session turned into a live porn act in front of a crowd of strangers. Why that thought aroused her and made her think of nothing more than taking him into a dark corner and having her way with his body she didn't know. She shook her head.

She felt the hands on her shoulders and an extra-large body press against her.

"Everything okay over here?" Trent asked. She closed her eyes and then turned toward him.

"Good," she whispered, voice sounding shaky.

"I'd better be sure," Trent said. His brown eyes sparkled with mischief as he leaned down and kissed her softly on the lips. His hand roamed across her ass and he pulled her tighter.

When he released her lips, she felt faint.

"Baby, I don't think I'm going to be able to stay here much longer. I need inside you. Deep, way deep into you." Her cheeks warmed as he pressed his hand under her hair and cupped the base of her head. He was going to kiss her again, and by the reaction her body had right now, she would orgasm right here by the bar.

"I need to use the ladies' room. Will you excuse me a moment?"

He leaned down and kissed her cheek. "You gonna run away from me, baby?"

She shook her head, but she was thinking, Hell yeah, so I don't come right here and moan loudly. "I need to go," she whispered. He scrunched his eyebrows together and that damn firm expression made her thighs quiver and her pussy ache. Damn, these men were so fine.

Making pies used to consume her every thought. Now suddenly, making love to Trent, Buddy, and Johnny together ruled her every thought. She shivered as she turned to walk away, and there was Buddy.

He took her hand, brought it to his lips, and kissed the top.

"Where ya going? My brothers scare you with their public display of possession?" he asked, then pulled her into his arms and held her around the waist with his hands locked behind her lower back. She held on to his forearms and smiled.

"They were being a bit wild, but I liked it," she admitted. He smiled.

"Good, because I give us about another twenty minutes tops and then we're out of here so we can get you home and make love for the rest of the night."

She hugged him and then looked back up at him. "I'll be right back, okay?"

He nodded and released her, but not before he gave her ass a light tap just as a group of guys was checking her out. She felt a little on edge as she passed the men gawking, but one look over her shoulder at Buddy's, Trent's, and Johnny's mean expressions toward the men had her feeling giddy inside. She waved at them and Johnny winked at her then watched her ass as she headed toward the bathroom.

Nina waited in a short line. It was pretty damn crowded in there. She finally got into the ladies' room, did her business, then looked at her reflection in the mirror. She looked so healthy and vibrant. She knew it had to do with her men. Tonight she was going to be completely honest, put all her fears behind her, and tell them how much she loved them.

She turned to head out of the ladies' room and back into the very crowded bar when someone bumped into her.

She looked at the blonde, hair all done up, lots of makeup, her breasts pouring from a two-sizes-too-small red tube dress she wore, and the woman smiled. Nina's gut instincts kicked in and put her on guard.

"Hi, I know you don't know me and are new around here, but as a woman, I felt it necessary to kind of give you a warning," she said.

Someone else bumped into Nina and she was forced to move closer to the wall. The young woman moved with her.

"Warn me?" Nina asked.

"Those guys you're with, they're bad news, and they can't be trusted."

Nina's heart started pounding. She gave the woman an expression that told her she wasn't buying her shit, but then the woman hurried to continue.

"Johnny, the paramedic, is a playboy. He picks up women all the time as a paramedic. I've heard that he does them right there in the back of the ambulance."

Nina was shocked, and she started having those funny, insecure sensations in her gut.

"He was charged with sexual harassment months ago for trying his playboy shit on some unsuspecting patient he responded to a call on. I'm just telling you that he and his brothers like to use women. They say how they haven't met anyone like you or haven't had sex in a long time, but they are full of shit. Believe me, my friends have had the misfortune of falling for their lies. They even have bets going as to how many women they can fuck. Johnny has a board right in the back of the ambulance. It's sick. I just wanted to warn you." She looked Nina over. "You seem sweet. Too sweet to be pulled down by such losers like them."

Nina was shocked and confused and didn't want to believe what this woman said when she pulled out her cell phone.

"Don't believe me about the sexual harassment charges?" She showed Nina her cell phone and a newspaper report about Johnny being accused of sexual harassment and getting suspended from the job.

Nina didn't know what to think or to do as she turned around, unsure where the exit was. She hurried out of the bathroom and away, away from the men, the woman who'd just ruined her night, never mind her life and her happiness, and she ran toward the door.

Just before she got there, Michaela was there, along with Hal. "Nina, what's going on? Where are you going?" she asked. Nina looked at Hal then at Michaela.

The tears filled her eyes. "I'm leaving. I don't believe this is happening."

"What is it? Is something wrong?" Hal asked, stepping closer.

Michaela looked around as if trying to see someone. Maybe she was looking for Trent, Johnny, and Buddy.

"I need to go. Some woman just told me all about Buddy, Trent, and Johnny and how Johnny is a playboy who uses women and how he was arrested for sexual harassment. They've been using me." Nina pulled away and headed out the door.

"No, Nina, wait!" Michaela said.

* * * *

"Hal, go get the guys and tell them what happened. I think Tara Kelly got a hold of Nina and told her those lies," Michaela said, and then she spotted Tara standing there flirting with some guys as she sipped her drink. She looked all smug.

Michaela headed her way. "Michaela. Michaela, don't do anything stupid," Hal said. Michaela could see the guys as well as Cindy, Serefina, and Jake coming toward them. Hal was waving toward Jake, Buddy, Johnny, and Trent.

Michaela approached Tara. "Hey, you. I think you need to relocate."

Tara looked her over and gave her a sassy look. It aggravated Michaela to no end. This lying, manipulating bitch had just hurt Nina with lies, and Michaela wasn't going to let her destroy that love she had with Trent, Buddy, and Johnny.

"What are you talking about?" Tara asked, and her friends stepped away, not even wanting to back her up. The guys watched and waited to see what would happen.

"Michaela, don't bother with her," Hal said and went to grab her wrist gently.

Michaela pulled it away. "No, she's a lying, manipulating little bitch with such low self-esteem that she needs to put down other women who are obviously better than her."

"Like who? That little nobody you're friends with? She's a street rat. She doesn't even have a family," Tara said. Now it appeared everyone was disgusted with Tara.

"She does have a family, and a hell of a lot more friends than you'll ever have. Now if you know what's good for you, you'll haul your skanky little ass out of here right now or the next charges you press against someone will not be a lie. They'll be for assault. Me assaulting you."

Tara's eyes widened, and she looked so scared. Michaela wanted to laugh, but she held her ground, hoping the woman would try something.

"You're crazy. That woman is a loser. I'm better than her."

In a flash, Tara was covered in some red tropical drink, and she screamed from the shock of it. Michaela looked to her left and there was Cindy.

"That's your last warning. You stay away from our friend Nina, and you stop spreading lies about Trent, Johnny, and Buddy or the next thing that will hit you is my fist," Cindy threatened.

Tara growled, then grabbed her bag and ran from the scene. Around them people cheered, and they could hear everyone yelling things to Tara as she left, like "don't come back," "loser," and "Nina."

Michaela turned toward Cindy, and Cindy raised her hand for a high five. "You go, girl. I didn't think you had that in ya."

They slapped hands and Jake pulled Michaela back against him.

"You and I are going to have a discussion about causing bar fights and public disturbance."

She chuckled. "I'll take whatever punishments you deem necessary, Sheriff."

"I am so glad I got all that on video," Tasha stated.

"Me, too," they heard others say.

They all laughed.

"Where are Johnny, Trent, and Buddy?" Michaela asked.

"They ran to find Nina. I hope they do. What a terrible misunderstanding," Cindy said.

"She's probably so hurt right now. I hope they find her fast. She's special," Bear stated.

"That she is." Jake squeezed Michaela a little tighter.

* * * *

Nina was so upset. She didn't know what to believe. Her thoughts were scattered into a thousand directions. What if what the woman said was true? What if the guys had used her and were only after her for her body and for a good time? Could Johnny really have a chart in the ambulance with check marks as to how many women he had sex with in there? The article had to be real. He was charged with sexual harassment. How could he do something like that? He was so sweet and compassionate. It just didn't make sense. The three of them did say they hadn't been intimate with anyone in a long time. Was that a lie, too, just like the blonde had told Nina? How could she stay in Treasure Town? How could she face all these people and try to open a business after these men hurt her like this?

She was getting angry now as she paced the parking lot. She looked around, still seeing people entering the bar, and then something caught her eye just as she was about to start walking.

It was the teenager with the baseball cap and red jersey. Why was he here? What was he carrying?

She felt her chest pounding. If she had a cell phone, she would call someone for help. But that was something else she didn't have and couldn't afford. Could Johnny, Trent, and Buddy actually like her because she was weak, had nothing, and was desperate to become part of something real?

She swallowed the lump of emotion in her throat as she hid behind the car and then walked closer. She could see him setting something up by the Dumpster. That teenager and Dumpsters didn't mix well if his past actions were proof. She needed to stop him. He was going to set the Station on fire. People were going to get hurt or worse. Johnny, Trent, and Buddy were in there.

She took a deep breath and headed toward the teen.

"Hey, what are you doing?" she called to him. He looked up and lit a lighter. "Don't do it!" she yelled.

"Nina!" She heard her name and saw Trent, Buddy, and Johnny heading around the front of the building.

"It's the arsonist. He's setting a fire!" she yelled to them. The kid was going to light the explosives. Nina ran forward, desperate to stop him from hurting any more people. She didn't know what came over her. Maybe it was the anger at the night's events, perhaps being accused of aiding the arsonist when she first met Trent, Johnny, and Buddy, or perhaps the simple fact that she was falling in love with Treasure Town and all its people. But whatever it was, she ran as fast as she could and she tackled the teenager. The lighter went flying, a small fire started, she saw out of the corner of her eye some flames and then someone stepping on them. Her body slammed against his so hard the kid yelled out and then rolled on top of her, trying to get away. She swung at him and he swung at her, ripping her dress, but then he was suddenly off of her, yelling out in pain. She looked to see Trent shove the kid against the concrete wall. Johnny was now next to her, leaning over her as she remained lying on the ground. He looked so concerned, so caring, but then came the thoughts of what he had done and the lies they told her.

"Goddamn it, Nina. What the hell were you thinking? My God, baby, are you okay?" Johnny asked her as he started checking her over.

"Is she okay?" Buddy asked, sounding breathless as the sounds of sirens in the distance came closer, and then people started crowding around the area.

She saw flashes, cameras going off, and then deputies arriving.

"I'm fine. Let me up." She cringed as both Buddy and Johnny helped her.

"Is she okay?" Trent called from across the way. The teenager was in handcuffs and looking a bit bloody. Trent looked so angry and intense as she locked gazes with him.

"She's okay. We're going to check her over now," Johnny said as the paramedics arrived.

She pulled her arm from his grasp. "I'm fine," she whispered.

Johnny looked shocked. "Nina, let me explain."

"I don't want to hear it, and I don't want to be added to your list of women you fucked in the back of your ambulance, okay?" she whispered and turned away.

"What?" Johnny asked. Michaela, Serefina, Cindy, and Tasha approached along with Jake, Hal, Bear, and a bunch of other friends.

"Nina, are you okay? My God, you caught the arsonist. He was going to try and blow up the Station." Michaela pulled her into a hug. Nina moaned.

"You're hurt," Cindy said. Nina glanced at Johnny's shocked expression and look of frustration.

"Hey, that woman inside, Tara, whatever she told you was a lie."

"Tara? Tara spoke to Nina?" Johnny asked.

"We took care of her, Johnny. She won't be spewing her lies anymore around here," Cindy added. They started telling Nina about what happened. With every detail and explanation about the false charges and the woman's obsession with Johnny and Trent and Buddy, Nina felt like shit. Her gut twisted. Her heart shattered. She didn't deserve such great men. Not with her past and her insecurities fucking up a good thing. She lowered her head.

"I want to go home." But even as she said those words, home didn't real feel like the right word to describe the apartment. There were no longer instant feelings of belonging. She felt like crap, plain and simple.

"I need to ask you some questions, Nina. Can you come over here to the patrol car? I'm Mercury, a paramedic, and I'll check you over to be sure that you're okay." She eyed the young guy, and he smiled as he followed her toward the deputy car.

* * * *

Johnny watched Mercury look over Nina. The fact that his friend and fellow paramedic got to touch her and undo her dress in the back to bandage up a small scratch that looked minimal was making him crazy. She actually believed what Tara had told her. She believed that he would keep tabs of women he had sex with in the back of the ambulance. Hell, he may have had sex back there once or twice years ago as a cocky guy who didn't care who he picked up because it was meaningless, but he sure never made a habit of it. He wasn't so insensitive. It was kind of like firefighters having sex with a woman on the top of a fire truck or a cop taking his woman up against the back of a patrol car.

He shook his head. Of course she would see that as chauvinistic and sexist. No wonder she stormed out of there and was so upset. He had to explain even though the women already told her the truth about Tara and what happened. Johnny had to make Nina see how important she was to him and to his brothers.

"She's really upset. I can't believe she ran and tackled that guy. My God, what was she thinking?" Buddy said as he ran his fingers through his hair.

"She was thinking about all the people who could have gotten hurt. She saved lives tonight. She loves this town."

"As soon as we get her home, we'll explain it all."

Mercury finished up and Trent pulled her into his arms and hugged her. She wrapped her arms around him and it gave Johnny hope that maybe she would understand and forgive him for what happened tonight.

* * * *

Nina was tired and just wanted to leave, especially after Tasha showed her the video of Cindy and Michaela telling off Tara. Tara had lied. About the sexual harassment and about Johnny using her, and it was obvious the woman had set Nina up and was obsessed with the men. Nina could understand their anger. She could also understand how upset Johnny was now to think that Nina believed the lies.

"Baby, you ready to head home?" Trent asked, wrapping an arm around her waist. She nodded and they said good-bye as everyone hugged her, including Burt and Jerome, who thanked her for saving their bar and all the patrons in it. They were really nice men and another part of what made this town so special.

The truck ride home was quiet. No one said a word and Nina was relieved right now because she really didn't know what to say. She just wanted to climb into bed and put the covers over her head. She had been so quick to believe some woman's lies and she knew why. She was waiting for something to go wrong, for something to arise to indicate that these three men were not as perfect and as much of a godsend as she needed, believed, and wanted them to be. And why? Because she was madly in love with them and thinking it could all fall apart, and they could leave her hurt worse than anything that ever occurred in her life.

They followed her up to her apartment, and the moment they got inside she turned around to face them.

"When that woman told me those lies, when she showed me that article and said that the three of you were using me, I thought I was going to die from the pain. It was what I had been waiting to hear. For someone to make reality come crashing down into my face and tell me that this isn't a perfect relationship. That the three of you were not sent down from heaven just for me, to make me feel loved, cared for, and part of a family. I'm sorry I believed it and allowed my own insecurities to dictate my reaction. I continue to battle on a daily basis, and that I made the decision to believe her and run off. The truth is that no matter how scared this makes me to admit, no matter what may come of us—if there still is an us—I absolutely positively love the three of you so damn much it hurts inside. I was so scared to tell you, to show that vulnerability, because it meant that you had a power over me, and if you left me, gave me up, didn't love me like I love you, then I would suffer and die from the pain. I don't want to sound like some obsessed psycho, but I don't think I could live without the three of you in my life, by my side. I need you and love you."

"We love you, too, Nina. Don't you think we feel the same fear that you would leave us and that this relationship could fail?" Trent asked. He walked forward and pulled her into his arms. "I love you, and it makes me so happy to know that you love me. You scared the hell out of me tonight." He squeezed her tight and she hugged him back.

Then she felt Buddy move in behind her. He pushed her hair aside and kissed her shoulder. "I love you, too. What you did tonight was so brave, but it also shows just how much you love this town and its people. This is your home now, Nina. We're your home and you're ours." He kissed her cheek and she turned toward him and he kissed her deeply.

When Trent let her go, he turned her around to face Johnny. Johnny's arms were crossed in front of his chest and he looked upset still. "I don't have a list in the back of the ambulance with names of women I fucked there."

She swallowed hard.

"I didn't assault or sexually harass Tara or any other woman ever. She wanted to sleep with me. I turned her down over and over again, and she became desperate for my attention. You are the only woman in my life that I love and want to spend the rest of my life with."

She smiled.

He reached out and pulled her toward him by her dress. She pressed her palms to his chest and he pressed his palms to her ass.

"Don't you ever place yourself into that kind of danger again. He could have seriously hurt you. You could have gotten burned or worse. Do you understand?"

She nodded her head and then laid her cheek against his chest.

"I love you, Nina. I love you more than anything in this whole world, and when I thought you hated me and wanted our relationship to end, I was sick with sadness and my heart felt empty. I didn't like that feeling. I never want to feel that again."

She pulled back and looked up at him. Her head tilted back to her shoulders to lock gazes with him. "Kiss me, Johnny, then take me to bed. I want to feel you, all three of you, inside of me."

"With pleasure, Nina," he whispered and kissed her.

* * * *

Johnny took his time undressing Nina after carrying her to the bedroom. He unzipped her dress while his brothers discarded their clothing and watched from the edge of the bed. He turned her toward them and slowly parted the material of her dress and let it fall. His brothers' eyes widened and sparkled with desire. He leaned forward to kiss her skin and of course the bandage over the scratch on her back. When he reached underneath her to cup her full breasts and play with the nipples, Nina raised her arms up and back against his neck and shoulders. The move caused her breasts to press forward. He trailed his palms down her belly and over her panties, pushing them down her thighs. She wiggled her hips and stepped out of them just as he stroked fingers along her pussy lips.

"Mmm." She moaned.

He pressed her closer to the edge of the bed and between his brothers.

"Put one leg on the bed, like you're going to straddle Buddy."

She did and Buddy leaned forward and caressed her inner thigh. She moaned again and Johnny moved his hands back up to her breasts, cupping them. Nina rocked her hips forward and Buddy pressed fingers to her cunt.

"She's so wet and hot. Ready for cock, aren't you, baby?" Buddy asked.

"Yes." She moaned, still holding on to Johnny's neck.

"I want you to keep your hands up, Nina, you hear me?" Johnny asked.

"Yes."

He stepped back, and she needed to balance herself on one leg, while keeping her hands up and back while he undressed. Trent stroked his cock and watched her as he scooted forward and ran the palm of his hand along her left hip and to her ass. He stroked down the crack and Nina shook, trying to maintain her balance.

"I want you to straddle Buddy. Take him inside of you and show him how fucking horny he makes you." He pressed her over Buddy's body as Buddy leaned back and helped her up. Her hands pressed over his chest to his shoulders and she took Buddy's cock right up into her cunt.

Buddy grunted. "Fuck yeah." She began to ride Buddy. Johnny watched her ass push back, and she widened her stance over Buddy to accommodate his thickness.

Up and down she thrust on him and threw her head back, moaning louder and louder. Johnny's cock twitched to be inside of her but he needed to make her understand how important she was to them, to him.

Johnny ran his hands over her ass cheeks and stared at her sexy, beautiful ass. "You need to know that we're never going to let you go, Nina. You're part of us. You belong to me and my brothers. Do you understand how much we love you and how deeply you're a part of us?" he asked. She moaned but didn't answer.

"Nina?" he questioned.

"Yes," she whispered as she continued to thrust on top of Buddy.

Smack.

"Oh!" Nina moaned.

"That's right. You answer me when I ask you a question, Nina. You belong to us. Isn't that right?" he asked her, and Buddy was obviously getting more aroused as he thrust up into her harder, faster, causing her reply to sound hesitant.

Smack.

"Oh God, yes. Yes, Johnny, I belong to you. To the three of you."

Smack.

"Fuck, that's hot." Trent reached out to cup Nina's breasts. He leaned forward to lick the nipple as she thrust on top of Buddy faster.

Johnny caressed her ass cheeks and spread them wider.

"Take Trent's cock into that sexy little mouth of yours, Nina, before I fuck this ass," he said.

"Holy fuck, you better stop talking and start fucking her before I come. I can't take this. Her pussy is clamping down on my cock," Buddy complained. Trent and Johnny chuckled.

Smack.

"Oh." She moaned and then shook. Nina came.

Johnny smacked her ass again and then pressed a finger to her anus.

"No more orgasms unless I say so, Nina. Now suck his cock," Johnny ordered. Nina opened wide and took Trent's cock into her mouth as if she were starving. Trent's hands locked onto her hair and head as he pumped his hips forward and Nina took him deep.

Johnny thrust his fingers into her ass as Buddy fucked her faster.

"Now, Johnny. She's ready," Buddy stated.

Johnny pulled his fingers from her ass, leaned down, and licked her anus. He kept stroking back and forth as she moaned.

"Damn, baby, that mouth of yours. Fuck." Trent carried on as he gripped Nina's hair and he moved back and forth against her mouth. She sucked and moaned, Buddy grunted, and Johnny knew she was ready. He tested her anus once again, being sure she was wet enough for his cock. He wasn't going to be able to go slow. He wanted to infuse his love and desire into her and aligned his cock with her anus. He felt so wild but he wanted to be sure not to hurt her. She was so willing and giving of her heart and her body to them, he wouldn't take advantage of that or distort her sweet sincerity.

He pressed the tip of his cock to her anus and she pushed back, taking him slowly into her ass. He held on to her hips, her luscious ass swallowed up his cock, and in no time, he was fully seated inside of her. He stared at his hands on her ass, against her creamy skin. He stroked his thumbs along the crack and her lower spine as he penetrated deeper. His hands were huge compared to her petite body. It aroused him, hardened his cock, and made him feel possessive and protective of her. He never wanted her to feel any pain or any sadness ever again and that overwhelmed him. He was in love, in lust with Nina. In and out he began to set a pace with Buddy. He could feel her body tighten and knew she was trying to give as good as she was getting. That was Nina.

"I love this ass. I fucking love fucking this ass, Nina."

Smack.

"Oh fuck, Johnny."

Buddy growled out as he shot his load and held himself up inside of Nina.

"Here I come. Damn," Trent stated next and held on to Nina and came. Nina swallowed him and moaned until Trent pulled from her mouth, cursing, and fell back onto the bed.

Johnny lifted Nina up and Buddy pulled out and moved out of the way. Johnny pressed her back down to the bed reached underneath her to stroke her pussy while he thrust into her ass. "Oh, Johnny, Oh God, this is wild." She gripped the comforter. His balls slammed against her ass, the bed shook, and he held her tight. She pushed back against his cock and he moaned.

"Please, Johnny. Please, I need to come. Please," she begged him.

He had been so far lost inside of her he completely forgot about telling her she couldn't come until he said so. "Fuck, I love you, Nina. Hold on. Just a little longer." In and out he stroked her cunt and then he felt her press her own fingers to her pussy and that was it. His brothers made comments, cheered them on, and Johnny was there.

"Now, Nina. Come for me now." He rocked his hips, and she screamed out his name. He shot his load into her ass and continued to rock his hips as his thighs shook and dizziness overtook him. They fell to the bed, him half on the edge and Nina spread out on her belly. He slowly lifted up, kissed her ass, her back, and her shoulders as he pulled out. She moaned.

"Perfect," he whispered.

"Abso-fucking-lutely," she said, and they all chuckled then joined her on the bed.

Chapter 10

"I found her. No more fucking excuses, Rico. She's going to be ours," Martino told Rico over the phone.

He sat forward in his seat, his heart racing. "Where is she? How did you find her?" he asked. He wanted Nina so badly he started to shake.

"She's in New Jersey. A regular fucking town hero."

"A town hero?"

"She stopped some arsonist that was on the loose. Some kid who attended the high school and was pissed off about being passed up for a baseball scholarship to some college. He was setting fires at locations where school board members and teachers worked besides the school itself. A really sick kid. Her picture is all over the place. She looks incredible. I've got two of my men there now watching her. Looks like she's been busy."

"What do you mean busy?"

"From their perspective, she's got three boyfriends. Two in law enforcement and one paramedic. A lot of first responders as friends. The damn town is loaded with military and law enforcement. It's going to be tricky grabbing her."

"I want to be there. I want to be with her first."

"Not this time, Rico. You fucked up the first time. I'm running the show. You get the paperwork together for the clubs. I've got a jet on standby. We leave tonight for Puerto Rico with our woman. I've got a penthouse, top floor of the hotel there, reserved for us. If you want to be there when Miguel and I take her for the first time, then be on that plane waiting for us."

Rico went to speak, to protest, but Martino disconnected the call. He slammed his fist down on the table.

She was fucking other men. He told her he would kill any man she fucked. But that was the least of his worries. He glanced at his watch. They were in New Jersey and getting ready to take her. He needed to fly out there, but he would never make it. Rico had planned for this. He needed to get to Puerto Rico. He would be there waiting in the penthouse. Then he could tell Nina why she needed to be loyal to him. She would finally know the truth and accept his possession of her. She had no choice.

* * * *

"These plans are coming along wonderfully. You have awesome ideas, Michaela," Nina told her.

"Me? What about you? I love the idea of having the large front porch where people can hang out and enjoy the place as well as the streets. It's a nice place to rest and have a slice of pie, some coffee, and enjoy the day."

"Exactly. I don't want it to feel like a fast-food place. You know, order, grab it, and get out."

"That's why it's going to be so special."

"I need to head over to Angel's Wings really quick and drop these pies off with Fannie. Then I'm having dinner with the guys. Johnny is supposedly cooking his famous chicken Marsala."

"Oooh, I've heard that it is pretty tasty. A nice romantic evening with your men. Enjoy it. Are you sure you don't need a ride over?"

"Definitely. I could use the exercise after taste-testing some new recipes with Cindy."

Michaela laughed and waved good-bye.

Nina traveled down the road. It was getting dark just as she got to Angel's Wings. She dropped off the pies and told Fannie she needed to hurry up and get back home, that Johnny was cooking dinner. She smiled and waved good-bye as Nina hurried down the road on her bike. She had just gotten to the long strip of road at the end of the block when she noticed a guy sitting on the sidewalk, slumped over. Cautiously she slowed down and then came to a stop. "Hey, are you okay?" she asked. She looked around for a pay phone but only saw a black sports car sitting there. She wondered if the guy was drunk. She didn't step closer.

"Hey, are you okay?" she asked louder. A hand came over her mouth from behind as someone pulled her off the bike. It fell to the ground, and she kicked and screamed, trying to get away from the man's hold. The guy on the ground stood up, smiling.

"Get her in the car before someone sees," he ordered. The man carried her to the car and got her inside. She tried crawling across the small backseat to the other door, but he grabbed her hips, pulled her back, and half sat on her.

"Hurry up and drive. Martino is at the airport waiting."

"Yeah, he just texted me. Somehow Rico is there, too."

Rico? Oh God, no. No, this can't be happening.

Nina tried to get the man off of her as the car sped out of the area. She was screaming, trying to use all her strength to get him off of her, but she couldn't.

The man gripped her tighter and pressed the gun to her face.

"I'll fucking knock you out, bitch, if you keep this shit up. Now cooperate, and maybe the bosses and his buddies will take their time breaking you in."

Bosses? Breaking me in? Oh God, they're going to force themselves on me. Oh God. Johnny, Trent, Buddy, please help me. Oh, please find me. Somebody help me. This can't be happening. Not now. Not when I've gotten this far.

Nina cried as the sports car got onto the highway that led straight out of Treasure Town. Her life was over.

* * * *

"Where the hell is she? Who could have taken her?" Buddy asked Jake as they searched the area where one of the deputies had found her bike.

"We're getting the surveillance footage from the corner store. Hopefully that tells us something," Jake said.

Johnny and Trent were standing there now, too. Jake's phone rang.

"Yeah, Rye." Jake repeated what Rye was telling him. "The feds seized their accounts and have control of a private jet scheduled to leave thirty minutes ago for Puerto Rico. Nina was on the list as a passenger for that flight."

"Fuck," Johnny yelled out.

"Who are these guys?" Jake asked Rye. Jake put the phone on speaker.

"Okay, my guy says that these two men, Miguel and Martino, are big-shot criminals from Puerto Rico. They're conducting a deal with Rico."

"Rico? Oh God, no. No, he found her, Rico has Nina," Johnny carried on.

"What else do you have? A location where they're keeping Nina?" Jake asked.

"I'm working on it. I can tell you that these men are not going to get out of the state, never mind the country. The feds are ready to arrest these three men and charge them with multiple counts of illegal gambling, prostitution, smuggling, and money laundering, never mind failure to report income and pay their fucking taxes. These guys are bad news. The feds and state police have all their locations of business under siege, their bank accounts, everything. It appears that they were planning on taking Nina to Puerto Rico with them and settling some business deal there. The state police have the two men who abducted her in custody."

"Any idea whatsoever as to where they might be?" Trent asked.

"The chatter from my source says they're checking hotels near the airport. I'd keep the scanners on and head that way if I were you," Rye told them.

"Thanks," Jake said and disconnected the call.

"Well?"

"Let's go. Let's head toward the airport. There's one hotel that is pretty close to it and a shuttle bus away from all terminals," Jake told them.

"If they hurt her, I swear I'm going to kill them," Johnny said as he got into the police cruiser with Jake, Buddy, and Trent. The deputies followed along with them.

* * * *

"There are fucking federal agents all over the place. We can't leave the fucking country," Rico told Martino and Miguel as they sat in a hotel room near the airport.

"Fuck, what's going on? We covered our fucking tracks," Miguel said as he paced the room.

Martino's cell phone rang and he answered it.

"What? Are you kidding me? That's what they told you? All right, stay by the jet." He ended the call. "The fucking airline won't let us take off. The jet is being looked over by federal agents right now."

"What are we going to do with her?" Miguel asked, turning toward the bed where Nina was tied to the headboard. Her mouth was taped closed, her wrists bound. She was staring at them wide eyed.

Rico walked over and sat on the bed. He ran the palm of his hand along her belly. "We could enjoy her for a bit until this shit passes. The feds aren't going to find anything on that jet. They can't keep us in the country without evidence, charges, a court order." He cupped her breast. Nina jerked and tried kicking her legs.

He eased over her. "Calm down, Nina. I told you that you belong to me."

* * * *

Martino walked closer and got onto the bed. He ran his hands along Nina's throat then down to her other breast. "She belongs to the three of us, Rico, perhaps only Miguel and me if this deal falls through," he threatened.

Rico felt his temper flaring. Nina was his woman. She always had been. Being forced to share her with these two was going to be a living hell. He watched as Martino leaned down and licked her neck.

He pressed her blouse open and smiled. "I didn't realize how big her tits are." Nina wiggled and shook but he held her firmly and Rico saw red. He wasn't sure he could go through with this. Seeing another man touch her, have his way with her, was torture.

"You look a little peaked, Rico. Maybe you should step out for some fresh air while Martino and I get to know Nina a little better," Miguel told him. It was an order. Rico wasn't stupid.

He slowly moved away from the bed. Martino licked across her nipple then tore open her blouse. He could see Nina's face, her eyes filled with tears. She was petrified. As Miguel joined Martino and began to rub his palm between her thighs, his anger grew.

"Leave, Rico. It's time for us to have some fun." Martino pulled out a knife and cut the ties where Nina's wrists were bound to the bed post. He pulled her down, and as she rolled to the side to get up and run, Miguel grabbed her around the waist and sent her back to the bed. He bent over her and thrust his hips against her ass as he chuckled and talked about fucking her from behind. Martino was pulling off his shirt and undoing his pants.

Nina struggled to get free, and she shoved at Martino, sending him to the side as she tumbled forward and off the bed with her own momentum. Martino grabbed for her, yanking her up by her hair, and Nina thrust a right hook at Martino's face. She turned and Miguel was there. He struck her in the face, pulled her up off the floor, and hit her again. Nina hit back and then wound up on the bed again. Martino stuck out his knife.

"You fucking want to fight us? I'll cut you, bitch. You'll learn to listen."

Rico couldn't take it any longer. Nina belonged to him. He pulled out his gun and fired, hitting Martino in the forehead. Miguel ran for his gun and turned just as Rico pulled the trigger and shot him in the chest.

He looked at Nina. She stood in the corner, shaking, only wearing shorts and a bra, her mouth still taped closed as she gasped for air. Her cheek was swollen, her arms bruised. She looked manhandled.

"Come to me, Nina."

She shook her head and cried out, snorting from the difficulty of breathing with the tape across her mouth.

"I'm not going to hurt you. I killed them for you. I stopped them from taking what's mine. Come on, Nina." He reached out, and when he touched her, she closed her eyes.

He pulled her against his chest and she continued to shiver and shake.

He put the gun back into his waistband and slowly reached over to pull the tape from her mouth. She gasped in pain and then cried out and bent over to breathe freely.

"We need to get out of here. Someone was bound to hear those shots. Come on now."

"No, Rico. I don't want to go. Why are you doing this to me?"

He grabbed her and pulled her against him. "You're mine, Nina. It's time you learn the truth and accept your fate."

She looked at him and he explained as he pulled her along with him.

They headed out of the room and toward the stairwell.

"I won you. I own you."

"Won me? What? You don't own me. Stop this craziness, Rico. I've had enough."

He jerked her against the wall and pressed his body firmly against hers.

"I do own you. Cleo paid his debt by giving me you."

* * * *

Nina was in shock. She shook her head side to side and tried pushing him away. But Rico wouldn't budge. He held her face firmly, and sweat dripped from his brow. She was perspiring, shaking, and bleeding. She couldn't believe what he told her.

"You didn't know him. I told you about Cleo," she replied.

"No, I pretended not to know him. He owed a lot of money on a bet he played and lost. He borrowed money from me. I'm a loan shark. It's what I do, and when you don't pay up, you owe money. He owed more than a hundred and thirty thousand. You were part of the payoff."

"Part of it?" she found herself asking as tears rolled down her cheeks. The realization that even the one man who helped to keep her off the streets and out of trouble had placed her into the arms of the worst trouble ever. She was disgusted, hurt, and angry.

Rico cupped her cheek, making the bruise ache more. He stared at her lips. "He couldn't pay up. His debt got higher, and he refused to hand you over. I had no choice, Nina. I wanted you." He covered her mouth and kissed her, cupped her breast, and squeezed her body. He was grinding his hips against hers and she shoved at him, parting their lips.

"No, no, it's a lie. He owed someone else money," she countered.

Rico shook his head and grabbed her wrist, pulling her down the stairs.

"No. He owed me and when he couldn't deliver or give me what I wanted and what he owed, he paid the ultimate sacrifice. His life."

Rico killed Cleo. Oh God, Rico killed Cleo. There's no way that Cleo would willingly give me to Rico to pay off a debt. He gave up his life for me.

They got downstairs to the exit and all the information was hitting Nina at once. But as they exited into the back parking lot, they saw all the police vehicles, including a sheriff's truck, and Trent, Buddy, Johnny, and Jake.

"Oh God!" she cried out.

Rico wrapped his arm around her waist and held the gun to her head. "I'll kill her. Let us go or she dies," he stated.

She locked gazes with Johnny, then Trent and Buddy, who had their guns out and pointed at Rico.

"There's nowhere for you to go, Rico. The place is surrounded. It's over," some guy in a suit said. She noticed the state troopers were there, too. They really were surrounded. This was a no-win situation and she had a feeling that she wasn't going to make it out of this alive.

Rico held tighter and backed up a little, but the door was closed.

"Don't move. Put down your weapon and we'll talk this through," the man in the suit stated.

"No talking. She's mine. I leave with her, dead or alive, I really don't care."

Suddenly the back door to the building flew open and the sound of gunshots filled the air. Nina dove to the ground and Rico was firing his weapon. The police fired theirs. She felt a sting to her arm and the ricochet of bullets by her head and body as they hit the pavement. She kept screaming and screaming even as the shots stopped and people surrounded her. Johnny, Trent, and Buddy were there yelling for an ambulance, asking for help. She saw their angry, concerned faces, and she twisted around to see Rico, bloody and dead on the ground, multiple bullet wounds to his body. Then she spotted Miguel, just as bloody, dead on the ground as troopers kicked his gun from his hand.

She realized that Rico had only shot Miguel once in the chest. He must not have killed him upstairs in the hotel room.

"You're going to be okay, baby. We're going to get you to the hospital," Johnny told her as he looked at her arm.

"I'm okay. Let me up." As she tried to move, she felt pain, a burning against her legs and knees. Her arm throbbed, and her face hurt.

"Fuck, she's all cut up!" Trent exclaimed.

The paramedics were there.

"I love you, baby. God, I'm so sorry we weren't there to protect you," Trent said as the paramedics helped to turn her over and place her onto the gurney.

She cried out in pain but somehow reached for Trent's hand. "I love you, too. This isn't your fault. But it's over now. It's all over."

He leaned down and kissed her hand. As the paramedics strapped her in and Johnny looked at the flesh wounds on her arms, his expression so serious, she smiled.

"I really was looking forward to that chicken Marsala of yours. Will you save me some?" She cringed as the paramedics lifted the gurney, making it shake. She closed her eyes.

"I'll make Marsala for you whenever you want, Nina, if you promise to not get into any more trouble ever again. I just can't handle it," Johnny told her as he leaned down and kissed her cheek.

She smiled and looked at Trent. "Now what fun would that be?"

"We'll talk about that comment later, Nina," Trent warned, and her heart lifted with confidence that a better life, a safer, happier life would now be achievable, with Rico gone and her past just as it should be, behind her.

* * * *

Six Months Later

Nina took a deep breath as she looked around her bakery. Everything was perfect. All the tables and chairs were set up and the display case looked exactly how she wanted it to, or at least for right now. Cindy yelled at her for changing it around a thousand different ways. She looked at her friends, who'd gathered around for the grand opening, and she smiled. A quick glance behind her and Nina saw that Cindy was by the counter, Mel by the register, and Michaela by the front entrance waiting for Nina's signal.

Nina looked at Buddy, Trent, and Johnny and smiled wide. "Well, this is it. The moment of truth."

"Go open the door, Nina, and let all those people inside. They've been waiting for hours for this grand opening," Johnny told her and she smiled. On shaky legs she walked to the door, flipped the sign from closed to open, and let the crowd in.

She greeted every customer, talked to them about her pies, about relaxing on the porch, and also about the recommendation box by the front door.

Before long the place was running smoothly after a few computer glitches that Trent helped with. She needed extra help behind the counter. Johnny helped with that. And finally Buddy helped her by placing the first twenty-dollar bill she earned as a new store owner in Treasure Town onto the wall by the register. She was so in love with them. They set her heart on fire and she would never be the same woman ever again.

She met other store owners on the block, took numerous catering orders for private parties, and even hired two other young women looking for part-time work. By the time the store closed and all her friends gathered around the tables, she was smiling wide and filled with energy.

"Aren't you exhausted, Nina? That was one hell of a grand opening," Cindy said.

"It sure was, but you know what? I'm so happy right now, filled with feelings of accomplishment and love," she said as she hugged

Trent while sitting on his lap. "And like I belong here, with my new family and friends. I'm blessed because of all of you, and because of Treasure Town," she said.

"We're happy for you, Nina. The pies were such a hit. This place is going to do fantastic," Jake told her.

"Hey, what kind of pie is this one?" Cindy asked. "I didn't try this one yet."

"Well, try it. It's something different."

"Different? Am I going to like it?" Cindy asked, looking concerned as she held the fork in her hand by the pie. Nina looked at Trent, Johnny, and Buddy.

They smiled and replied in sync.

"Abso-fucking-lutely."

THE END

WWW.DIXIELYNNDWYER.COM

ABOUT THE AUTHOR

People seem to be more interested in my name than where I get my ideas for my stories from. So I might as well share the story behind my name with all my readers.

My momma was born and raised in New Orleans. At the age of twenty, she met and fell in love with an Irishman named Patrick Riley Dwyer. Needless to say, the family was a bit taken aback by this as they hoped she would marry a family friend. It was a modern day arranged marriage kind of thing and my momma downright refused.

Being that my momma's families were descendents of the original English speaking Southerners, they wanted the family blood line to stay pure. They were wealthy and my father's family was poor.

Despite attempts by my grandpapa to make Patrick leave and destroy the love between them, my parents married. They recently celebrated their sixtieth wedding anniversary.

I am one of six children born to Patrick and Lynn Dwyer. I am a combination of both Irish and a true Southern belle. With a name like Dixie Lynn Dwyer it's no wonder why people are curious about my name.

Just as my parents had a love story of their own, I grew up intrigued by the lifestyles of others. My imagination as well as my need to stray from the straight and narrow made me into the woman I am today.

For all titles by Dixie Lynn Dwyer, please visit
www.bookstrand.com/dixie-lynn-dwyer

Siren Publishing, Inc.
www.SirenPublishing.com

Lightning Source UK Ltd.
Milton Keynes UK
UKOW01f0826090218
317586UK00007B/519/P